Jim and Tammy Bakker—
Public and Private

Mike Richardson was evangelist Jim Bakker's personal
bodyguard for nearly one year. During that time he saw
both the public and private sides of Jim and his wife
Tammy Faye.

He saw a man with seemingly boundless energy and cha-
risma, who inspired trust and faith in millions.

He saw a man who contradicted his own sermons against
drinking and drugs, who knowingly misrepresented the use
of thousands of dollars in donations.

He saw a woman whose talents and enthusiasm were an
important force in the success of the PTL ministry.

He saw a woman whose insecurities drove her to sudden
pettiness and callousness towards others, yet who at times
could display an unexpectedly appealing manner.

Mike Richardson was there for the Bakkers' fights and their
triumphs, for their hectic working days and their lavish
spending sprees. In *The Edge of Disaster*, he recounts his
year with the Bakkers.

It was a year that he will never forget.

THE EDGE OF DISASTER

Michael Richardson

ST. MARTIN'S PRESS/NEW YORK

THE EDGE OF DISASTER

ISBN: 0-312-91093-2   Can. ISBN: 0-312-91094-0

Printed in the United States of America

First St. Martin's Press mass market edition/September 1987

10 9 8 7 6 5 4 3 2 1

To my mother,
who has always been my best friend—

and to Mr. and Mrs. Jim Smith
and Mr. and Mrs. Dale Hawkinson,
for giving me the courage

and to Maria,
who knows why

ACKNOWLEDGMENTS

Thanks to Debbie Roman, for a fine job of transcription.

Thanks to Harriet, Jim, Susan, Will, Buffi, and W. van H.—each of them knows why.

And thanks to my publishers for all their help, especially for their contribution of the captions that accompany the photographs.

"When you're on the edge of disaster, you're really on the brink of a miracle."
—JIM BAKKER

I worked for PTL from November 1983 to October 1984. I was Jim Bakker's personal bodyguard, with the man for sixteen to eighteen hours a day. I drove his car, put his eight-year-old son to bed, helped oversee the guards who staffed the house at Tega Cay, went on the trip when Jim spent $100,000 on automobiles in two days—less than three months after attending the staff meeting in which Jim announced that he and Tammy had just put all their savings into the ministry.

I saw Jim receive an honorary doctorate from the college that he said had kicked him and Tammy out.

I saw him drink vodka, despite his stand against alcohol.

I saw him build and open a home for unwed mothers.

I saw him take Valium, despite his preaching against drugs.

I saw him ride his employees unmercifully.

I saw him collapse with exhaustion.

I never saw him visit his parents' house on the PTL grounds, nor did I ever see his parents visit his house. I never heard of such visits, either.

I heard and saw Tammy daily, and I will tell you how she was that year.

I knew David Taggart, Jim's personal assistant, who in his late twenties was making over $300,000 a year. It was David who gave Jim Valium in my presence. It was David who dispensed the unaccounted cash drawn by the president's office for Jim's travel.

I knew Richard Dortch, an Executive Presbyter of the Assemblies of God, who allowed $500,000 in remodeling and redecorating to be spent on his residence—and who wanted control of the PTL purse strings.

I knew Vi Azvedo, the Bakkers' personal counselor, who was credited within PTL with putting Jim and Tammy's marriage back together after a separation. Vi was in charge of the PTL marriage counseling workshops—which did a great job, by the way.

She also mixed Jim's vodka and orange juice.

I saw the place where the wife-swapping happened, and I was told who the swappers were.

They weren't Jim and Tammy.

The Bakkers had nothing to do with it—except to put a stop to it the instant they heard about it and make the location where it occurred off limits to all but Security personnel.

I saw Jim send $100,000 to a burned-out church in Detroit—a church not affiliated with PTL in any way.

2

I heard Jim laugh at his followers, the very people who trusted him without question.

And I saw the donations flood in—forty or fifty trays of mail a day, each tray the size of a card table top, about 40 percent of the donations in cash.

I heard where Jim got the idea for financing the Heritage Grand Hotel by giving Lifetime Partnerships—and it wasn't from God, the way he said it was.

I never saw Jim read the Bible, except to find a line that would support what he'd already decided to say.

I saw Jim give $100,000 to the Good Will in Charlotte.

I never saw Jim pray, except in front of the cameras or with someone who'd asked him to pray with them.

I never saw a man as jealous of a woman as Jim was of Tammy.

I saw Jim, and Tammy too, do a lot of good things. A whole lot.

I saw it all. I lived it all.

CHAPTER 1

I was a stranger and ye took me in.

MARK 25:35

How did I join the PTL organization and become private bodyguard to Jim Bakker?

After I left the Marine Corps, I became a law enforcement officer in the sheriff's department of York County, South Carolina—the county in which most of PTL is located. Starting off as a uniformed deputy, I was promoted to detective, later to sergeant of detectives. Growing unhappy with law enforcement after eight years, I became a private investigator. I hoped to build a healthy business. As I soon found out, however, a private investigator is nothing more than a person who follows married people around to find out what they are doing. I loathed it.

In March 1983, I went to work for Tom McKinney, an attorney in Rock Hill, S.C., and his associate, Tom Givens. I was an investigator on their criminal and civil cases and a researcher on their real estate dealings. McKinney and Givens represented PTL in

South Carolina as far as real estate was concerned. When a tract of land was to be bought, I would research the property back some sixty years to clear the title.

Some time before 1978, Bakker, evidently outgrowing his location on Park Road in Charlotte, N.C. (the city limit was some two miles from PTL), had bought a large tract of land, some 1500 acres, which had been partly developed for an industrial park that never came into being. Some roads had been cut and some sewer lines had been laid. As a policeman, I'd been all too familiar with the tract; before Bakker bought it, it had been a haunt of drug dealers and a mausoleum of stripped cars.

Now, in 1983, he was filling in around the tract; PTL was buying a lot of land, farms of twenty acres here, a hundred acres there—really gobbling it up.

It fell to me to take papers over there for signature or approval and to deliver deeds and titles when the work was completed.

In the spring of 1983 the Heritage Grand didn't exist, except in Jim's mind, but PTL was already booming. I'd been there in late 1981, when PTL had finished paving the roads and had built the barn that was Heritage Village Church. It was also where Bakker did the shows. The building seated 2500 to 3000, depending on how the seats were arranged, and it looked just like a big barn with a stone, one-story reception area tacked on the front. In late 1981 PTL was completing the rustic, one-story Registration Center and the ultramodern, glass-and-stone, pyramidal Outreach Center. It had looked good then. Now, in spring 1983, it looked even better. They had built and sold about a hundred one-story garden duplexes in an area called Dogwood Hills, creating a whole residential neighborhood, and they had more units going up all the time. They had built six vacation chalets behind the Registration Center, on the lake, and a 3500-seat outdoor amphitheater. The 500-site campgrounds were in operation, and the Upper Room, a prayer center, was up.

More than once I took papers up to Bakker's office, on the third floor of the Outreach Center. Actually, the president's office *was* the third floor of the Outreach Center.

Carpeted in off-white throughout, the third floor had Jim's private office, Tammy's private office, a dining area and kitchen, the boardroom, two offices unoccupied at that time, and David Taggart's office. The floor wrapped around a three-story tall atrium; hanging plants dangled down to the first floor.

I'd never heard anything bad about Bakker. At the sheriff's department, we never had any complaints. Of course, there were the jokes people make, but I never heard anything bad worth paying attention to. I thought a lot of him, when I thought about him at all.

Anyway, I'd go up to the third floor and deliver papers to Shirley Fulbright, his secretary. It was really pretty up there, with glass-and-brass tables, white walls, paintings of country scenes and religious subjects, and Israeli artifacts. Bakker had been in Israel in 1981, doing a series of shows from the Wailing Wall, the Mount of Olives, and the Upper Room.

Jim's office had a lot of animals on the floor—

stuffed fabric animals and animals sculpted out of wood and metal.

Tammy's office was thickly decorated with dolls.

The whole floor had glass outside walls. You could pull curtains inside if the sun got too bright. Outside, the whole third floor was rimmed by a terrace which I rarely saw used.

The third floor—the president's office—was just beautiful. I felt it was a privilege to be there.

I felt I was in the office of somebody very special.

One day I saw Jim through his glass office wall. He was sitting at his desk in his shirt-sleeves, talking to some people. He was smaller and slighter than I expected from seeing him on television—five foot five inches or five foot six inches, about 150 pounds. I stood there a moment, wishing I could hear what he was saying, wishing I could just sit down and talk with him. I thought that would be a wonderful experience. I really admired that man.

During the spring I renewed my acquaintance with Don Hardister, PTL Chief of Security, whom I had met while I was with the York County Sheriff's Department. A threat had been called in late 1981: a bomb, the caller said, had been placed under the Barn, directly under the stage where Bakker would be doing the show. I went up there and crawled under the stage, through a real rabbit warren of little partitions and large, snaky cables. I found it: a kitchen-size matchbox with yellow and green wires sticking out of it, wrapped with gray duct tape. It looked very authentic; it turned out to be a fake. That was when I met Don for the first time; we'd talked on the phone from time to time since then.

* * *

In September of 1983, I began to think about other things to do. The money was not too good in the work I was doing. A friend in the sheriff's department suggested that I look at opportunities in private security, since I didn't want to go back into law enforcement. I liked the area, and wanted to stay there. So I contacted Don Hardister and he invited me up to talk to him. Don had been with PTL almost since the organization itself began.

Well, I hadn't been on the PTL grounds in a couple of months, and I was astonished at the changes that had taken place. They'd planted a lot of trees, done a lot of beautiful landscaping work.

Between forty and fifty more one-story garden duplexes had been built at Dogwood Hills, and the first model was going up at Mulberry Village, a planned development of single-family detached houses.

I was to meet Don at the Barn studio, so I went on out there. The Barn area had yet more surprises for me. They'd built the enormous (25,000 square feet) gray stone two-story Total Learning Center next to it, attached to the Barn with common doors.

The TLC, I'd learn, housed the Heritage Academy, which was the kindergarten-through-twelfth-grade Christian school. It was also used for the School of Evangelism and Communications, for offices, and for seminars and Sunday school. There was also a whole new, enormous stone studio on the back of the Barn.

The parking lot was large, and full of buses and cars of every description: old, new, small, expensive. I went inside the studio, into a lobby area that extended the full width of the building. It had several different seating areas, each with a TV set, and a few people talking or watching the PTL show. Most of them had Bibles in their hands. On the left was an information counter with several people behind it. I went over and asked for Don Hardister. They told me to go into the studio.

I opened the double door and was engulfed in the world of live television. To my right was a large bleacher section that was filled with over a thousand people. Straight in front of me was a smaller bleacher section, with about thirty people seated behind long desk-surfaces, most of them with phones to their ears. The others had their eyes glued to the stage area, which was decorated like a dream living room. The stage was elevated about a foot and was carpeted.

Off to the left of the stage was an area of many plants, some almost small trees, and some tables, a sort of garden, and to the far right of the stage was another stage area, where several men and women stood with microphones in their hands. These were the PTL Singers. To the right of them the band was seated in an elevated section.

And there on the main stage were Jim and Tammy Faye, side by side on a couch, with several people on the stage with them. Tammy Faye looked slimmer and more graceful in person than she does on television: the camera adds about ten pounds to a person and can make short people look squat.

Four or five cameras were in front of them in a concrete area between the stage and the audience. The guys at the camera controls worked with split-second precision movements, in and out, left and right. It was fascinating. To say the least, I was impressed!

Don saw me, came over, and led me behind stage, where the telephones were—the phones the Prayer Partners used to call in during the show.

We went down a wide corridor, about seventy-five yards to a locked, guarded door. I should say right here that there was good reason for locked doors and guards. At this time, and all during the time I worked for PTL, we received an average of four to six death threats a week. Don unlocked the door, and led me into Jim and Tammy's sitting area.

It was large and lavishly furnished, with a big white L-shaped sectional sofa, green carpet, and a contemporary beige coffee table with a white top where some brass deer sat. There was a Mitsubishi widescreen TV, some bookcases, and some very expensive-looking bronze and brass works. Also some carvings that looked like ivory.

Over to one side was Jim's desk, where he kept his sermons.

One wall was nothing but mirrors, bordered with lights, with a long dressing table in front of it and two or three stools. One door led off to Jim's dressing room, another to Tammy's.

Don sat me down. In his early thirties then, about my age, Don is around five feet eight inches tall, stocky, with receding light brown hair. He wore an impeccably trimmed beard. His clothes, although very neat, didn't go together quite right because Don suffers from some degree of color blindness. An ordained minister himself, he was very dedicated to Jim's ministry. He hated lawbreaking, and lawbreakers.

That day I could see the tiredness in his grayish blue eyes. He told me that he was under enormous pressure and had not slept in days. He said I was almost a godsend.

He had been looking for somebody to assist in the everyday operations of the PTL Security Organization, somebody who could also be with Jim Bakker some. He said that he had been with Bakker day in and day out for so long now that the day-to-day operations were suffering. He needed help.

Don asked, "Think you can handle the position?"

Everything I'd heard about PTL was good and everything I'd seen had impressed me. I thought I could be very proud to work for this religious organization and maybe build a future there. I liked Don, and he had an impeccable reputation. I went away, thought it over for a few days, and called Don.

My answer was yes.

Don was happy I'd decided to come, and said, "I need you to meet Jim, but I got to figure out a way to do it. I just can't take you up there and say, 'This is Mike Richardson, he's going to come to work for us,' because you'll have to be with him a great deal."

So before that day's show was over, Don took me to Jim's car, a Buick Park Avenue, put me in the backseat, and told me to wait. After half an hour he came back with Jim Bakker, who was wearing a three-piece suit, his hair still neatly combed from the show. I got a whiff of British Sterling as Bakker climbed in.

Bakker got in the front—where he almost always

sat unless he had a family member with him, I would learn. He was directly in front of me, but didn't seem to see me at all. Don got in, started the car, and we headed out.

He said, "Jim, I've got somebody in the backseat I want you to meet."

Four or five minutes of silence.

I thought, This guy isn't the caring person I thought he was. I would later learn this would be normal for Jim; after a show he would often be keyed up and sort of in another world.

Then Bakker talked some small talk with Don. He still didn't seem to be aware I was there.

Finally, Don said again, "Jim, I've got somebody in the backseat I want you to meet." He gave my name and credentials and added, "I would like him to come to work for us."

Bakker turned around. And all of a sudden there was this glowing expression on his face, a great smile that just took all of my bad feeling away. He stuck his hand out around the seat and said, "I'm Jim Bakker. Nice to meet you."

"Nice to meet you, sir."

He said, "Former police officer, huh?"

"Yes, sir, I have been in the past. I got out of it a year or so ago."

He stopped and looked at me. "Well, tell me something about yourself."

I said, "Well, I was in the Marine Corps, and I was a police officer . . ." and went on giving him my experience.

He said, "No, what religion are you?"

"I'm Baptist."

"Baptist, huh?"

"Yes."

He kind of laughed. "Well, all Baptists aren't bad." And he made some reference to Uncle Henry Harrison, who was brought up Baptist. He added, "I won't hold that against you." He turned back around and cut the conversation off completely.

Well, I thought, he's made up his mind against me because of that one fact. I already screwed up. There is no way this guy is even going to consider me. This being a job with a religious organization, I figured that sort of thing—what religion I was—might be real important to him. I mean, me, being a Baptist and he is a Pentecostal Holiness or whatever, there is no way I am going to get a job with him.

We took him over to his office, saw him safely to the third floor—where the security was very tight—and left.

The next day Don called. "I've got some good news. Jim liked you."

"That's hard to believe." I hadn't been able to tell whether he liked me or not. And I remembered his reaction to me being a Baptist.

"That's just the way he is, don't worry about it. Now, I would like you to come in and go through another interview with a lady by the name of Vi Azvedo. She interviews people before they are hired and is in charge of personnel."

I've never had such an interview in my life.

I waited in her office at the appointed time. In walked this heavyset older lady, probably in her late forties or early fifties. She wore her hair up on her head, all sprayed down like the style several years ago, in a kind of bunlike thing.

She asked me why I wanted to come to PTL, and I told her I needed a job and knew Don Hardister and all that.

She started digging. "Are you married?" No. "Have you ever been?" Yes, twice. I had been married for several months when I was twenty. I'd married again at twenty-three. That marriage had broken up in 1982, after six years. She asked did I and my ex-wife want counseling—was there any chance of a reconciliation? That took me aback. I said absolutely not.

Then she asked me, "Are you dating?"

I said of course.

And then: "Are you sexually active?"

I almost laughed at this outrageous line of questioning. Sure I was active, but she probably would have fainted if I told her how active. Then again, maybe she would have liked it.

I evaded the question. It was none of her business—or PTL's, either. What did this have to do with whether I could do the job?

Well, she gave me an application to fill in.

It asked, Was I saved? I said yes. I'd been baptized, in 1973. That's what the question meant to me.

Then it asked what it meant to me to be saved, and how I believed in Jesus Christ. Well, I put down something like, I believe in God and I believe people are forgiven if they repent, and that's why I got baptized, because that's what my religion calls for.

I don't remember exactly the words I put down.

All these questions about sex and religion made me feel raped, if I can put it that way.

I told Don I had been none too happy with this interviewing process, but he said, "In your case it's just a formality." *Formality, my ass,* I thought. *I bet she keeps files on this stuff—PTL's version of J. Edgar Hoover.*

In a couple of days he called and said, "When can you start?"

So, in October 1983, I became an employee of PTL. My starting salary was $22,000; by the time I left I was making $30,000. My title was Captain of Security, reporting directly to Don; later I would be Assistant Chief.

I could see why Don needed more people. The department was in disarray—Don had been trying to do the work of two or three men, and even he couldn't manage that.

At that time the department was about forty people. We had some 2000 acres to cover at PTL, with a lot of buildings, a lot of visitors, *and* a lot of cash donations in the mail—just a huge responsibility. Also, we had to have a staff out at the Bakker home in Tega Cay, some ten or twelve miles from the grounds of PTL.

In Charlotte there was the Park Road place, a mansion where PTL had really gotten its feet on the ground. It was used now as a guest house, and another building on the grounds was used for tape storage and editing and the production of the foreign-language versions of the shows. That had twenty-four-hour security, too.

The Park Road storage/editing building had a

great indoor swimming pool—tiled, just beautiful, like something out of Roman days. When I was shown it, I blurted, "What a great place to work out!"

"Don't ever come over here alone with a girl," my companion said. (I guess he thought I said "make out.")

"What? Why on earth not?"

"This is where the wife-swapping took place."

My companion told me that two couples had been involved in the incident, which had happened some years before. It was never suggested to me in any way that Jim and Tammy were involved—except in putting a stop to it the minute they heard about it. Two of the four people were still working for PTL in 1984.

Before all this happened, I believe the pool had been used for baptisms. Not anymore, it wasn't.

Pretty as it was, it was off limits to everyone while I was there. Only Security had keys to it—or so I was told.

But that conversation took place some months later. My first duty was to hire nine security guards and get them trained.

For my first couple of weeks I saw very little of Jim, except for the shows. Shows were taped every day, before 1000 to 1500 people. It was a rare day when attendance dropped as low as 600, even in the winter.

Jim put on a good show. Even I, with no show business experience, could tell that he had a real knack for talking on camera and for getting to people just by the way he talked.

I paid a lot of attention to the shows. They were

really impressive, all the cameramen and other professionals running around. It was like Hollywood in Fort Mill, S.C. I confess I didn't listen much, though, to what Jim was saying on the air.

After a couple of weeks, I began driving for Jim some days. I learned that it was part of my job to get him to the studio in the mornings in as good a mood as possible. I learned to make sure he had no bad experiences on the way, no traffic to startle him, nothing to scare him, because he startled very easily and he became upset very easily. I would get him to the studio and get him out of the car. He liked for people to open doors for him, but he surely didn't like people moving fast around him, especially if they were behind him. You had to almost telegraph what you were going to do so he'd know everything was okay. He moved pretty quickly himself, so it wasn't easy to get to a door before he did, but if you moved real fast to get ahead of him, it would scare him and he'd jump. More than once I saw him almost jump out of his shoes because somebody moved fast around him when he didn't expect it.

The way I started the driving was that one day, after the show, Don Hardister said to me that he thought it was time for me to just start being with Jim some.

He said, "Now, I haven't told him that you are going to be with him. What you are going to do when he comes out of the dressing room door, you just take him to his car and put him in and wherever he wants to go, you go with him." Don added details of what I was to do.

Jim didn't seem surprised to see me when he came

out in his navy blue suit. We pulled out of the garage. He didn't talk to me at all at first, except to give me directions. I felt kind of insulted.

He'd say, turn here, and I would almost miss the road (because he always left it to the last minute), but I would turn and he'd say stop here, and I'd stop, and he would just look. Finally we rode around to this field with a few trees in it, and he said, "This is where the hotel is going."

I was at a loss. I didn't know what he was talking about.

He looked at me and said, "This is where the Heritage Grand Hotel is going."

I said, "Yes, sir, that looks good to me."

He said, "Do you know what I'm talking about?"

"Well, no, sir, I'm sorry."

"Have you not been listening to my shows, what I have been talking about?"

I said, "Yes, sir, I have. I knew you were going to build a hotel, but I didn't know where."

"This is where it's going. It is going to be eleven acres under one roof. It is going to be the most magnificent thing you have ever seen." He said, "God told me to build it here, and this is what it is going to be. It is going to have five hundred rooms. Disney World is going to be nothing compared to this. If Walt Disney can do it, I can too. There has got to be a place for Christians to come to. People go to Las Vegas, Nevada, and they have the nicest places in the world to gamble. Why can't we have a place where Christians can be that is equally as nice? This has got to be. This has got to happen. This is the time for Christians to have a nice place

18

to go." He just loved the idea of the hotel. He loved to talk about it, almost as if he got high when he went over the details.

I said, "Yes, sir." He struck me as a man full of dreams—it sort of scared me, his dreams were so elaborate. They seemed too big for one man.

Suddenly he broke it off and picked up the two-way radio we had in the car, and said, "Unit 88 to unit 82." Unit 88 was us; unit 82 was David Taggart's call number. David was his personal assistant.

David picked up.

Jim asked, "What do I have today?"

"Well," said David, "you have a meeting in your office waiting on you."

That was the end of conversation with me for the trip. He'd jump from one subject to another, one person to another, extremely quickly, all the time I knew him.

I took him over to the Outreach Center and up to his meeting. He stayed there most of the afternoon.

As would become the custom, I waited around the Outreach Center until he needed me again. If he hadn't given me an assignment and David Taggart didn't want me doing something, I would be downstairs in the Security office doing paperwork or helping out where I could, but always standing by in case he needed me.

The first floor of the Outreach Center was where they counted the donations. Two couriers worked each shift, collecting mail from the post office twice a day, bringing it to the center for counting and then making the deposits. There was a walk-in safe—a Mosler—where they kept the money until deposit.

Tammy Faye also stored some of her furs and jewelry there.

It was something to see—all those envelopes. All that money. Millions of dollars of donations came in each month; in August 1984, I believe, PTL received twelve million dollars. I estimate at least 40 percent of the donations came in in cash.

I worried about security on the mail room all the time I was there. I was told that PTL had lost $50,000 to an employee before I came. They had fired her but had not pressed charges. They just took the loss. But we never had any trouble while I was there—nobody from outside trying a holdup, no theft from inside.

That first evening I took Jim home to Tega Cay. And from shortly thereafter, I was Jim's personal bodyguard, living with the family when we were on the road, working with him up to eighteen hours a day when we were at PTL. It was a very demanding job, looking after this immensely successful evangelist, sometimes larger than life—this hugely convincing, greedy, insecure, visionary, hard-driving, hard-driven man.

CHAPTER 2

The people which sat in darkness have seen a great light.

MATTHEW 4:16

Televangelists, some people call them: preachers who use television to spread the word of God, and to ask for money to continue God's work.

But that's the idea, and it's not so different from the minister passing the plate in Sunday morning services at home.

Except that the hometown preacher has a vestry, or board of elders, or board of deacons, or somebody making him account for every penny; and any member of the congregation can find out where the money goes. Every penny of it.

With Jim, even the IRS and the Justice Department are having a lot of trouble finding out. They've subpoenaed Jim and Tammy and seven others, according to the press, to deliver all records detailing financial and "employment activities" to a grand jury.

And a West Virginia couple, David and Sarah

Coombs, have filed a Federal lawsuit against Jim and Tammy, charging fraud and racketeering.

And PTL has filed for bankruptcy, despite the fact that Heritage U.S.A. is the third most popular theme park in the country, right behind Disneyland and Disney World.

You know, Jim said to me more than once that the reason he was in such a hurry to get Heritage U.S.A. finished was that sooner or later the Federal Communications Commission was going to slap some stiffer regulations on television about asking for gifts of money, and he had to get it built before that happened. His dream was to make Heritage U.S.A. self-sufficient, so he would no longer have to depend on television.

It seems to me that the way Jim ran PTL is going to make the FCC act faster than it would have otherwise. What an irony—and in August 1987, there's talk of an investigation of television ministries in the House of Representatives.

Before we get into the way religion was practiced at PTL, let me tell you what the religion was. It's a little confusing if you're outside it.

But even before that, what does *PTL* stand for? It stands for Praise the Lord, or People That Love—or simply stands on its own. (And of course there are the jokes—Pass the Loot and Pay the Lady.) I guess the best answer is that *PTL* stands for PTL.

Back to religion and the way it was practiced at PTL.

First of all, Jim is an Evangelical Protestant Christian.

Evangelical Protestants emphasize close attention

22

to the Bible, personal commitment to Christ, and missionary work. The Southern Baptists are the largest Evangelical denomination, with 14.6 million members, including Billy Graham and Jimmy Carter. This is the denomination I grew up in.

Until May 1987, when they dismissed him, Jim Bakker was a minister of the Assemblies of God, ordained on April 29, 1964. The Assemblies are one of the fastest-growing denominations in the country, and their membership is up 34 percent to 2.1 million members, since 1975.

Jim grew up in the Assemblies of God. In fact, his grandfather Joe Bakker founded and helped build Creston Gospel Tabernacle, the first Assembly of God church in Muskegon, Michigan (Jim's hometown), in 1923. Grandparents on both sides of his family were charter members.

Jim, like the Assemblies, is Pentecostal. Pentecostals place great importance on direct communication with God, and on gifts of the Holy Spirit, such as the power to heal, personal prophecy, and speaking in tongues.

People who speak in tongues believe that the Holy Spirit is visiting them, that the Lord is speaking through them. What they say is sometimes in Greek or Swahili or some other language that the speaker has no way of knowing, or so the belief is. Sometimes what they say is in no known language—although it often sounds like the way Indians sound in the movies—but those who believe in it believe it is an important religious experience. They believe that what is said is a message directly from God. That's the way I understand it, anyway.

Speaking in tongues and the name *Pentecostal* itself come from the account of the Pentecost given in the Bible in the second and third chapters of Acts, where the Apostles received the gift of tongues. Many wonders and signs were done by the Apostles and three thousand were baptized—well, you can read it yourself.

The study of the Bible is less important to many Pentecostals than the direct gifts of the Spirit—not that it's unimportant, I wouldn't want to suggest that for a minute. It's just that it may be the difference in emphasis that accounts for the fact that I never saw Jim study the Bible. Oh, he'd check it for quotations that would support what he'd already decided to say—but I never saw him sit down to study it. Then again, maybe he felt he knew it so well already that he didn't really need to study it.

It seems odd, though, that I never saw him pray unless he was with people who'd asked him to pray with them. Or on camera.

Once Jim did go to a small room at the Upper Room to pray behind closed doors. He had announced on television that he was really going to wrestle with the Lord in prayer.

Jim was in there for about fifteen or twenty minutes.

He said he was going to pray in private there each day for a whole week, but I only remember him doing it for one day.

He didn't say grace at meals even, not in my presence, unless he was in a public area of a restaurant at Heritage U.S.A. or with people he didn't know very well.

Once the subject of faith healing came up. Vi Azvedo said, "Jim, you really ought to consider doing some healing on the show."

Jim answered, "Yeah, but what if it doesn't work?"

Jim did do faith healing off camera, after the show, when he'd stick around and talk to the audience. But the healing was always very general: "I feel that someone here is suffering from back problems," for instance; and then several hands would go up because a lot of the people were over forty, and he'd pray and say something like, "I feel the power of God healing you even as I speak."

Two or three times I saw the casting out of demons after the show. There'd be a whole group of ministers then, Vi Azvedo, Dr. Fred Gross, Frank Marklin, perhaps Uncle Henry Harrison, and Aimee Cortese.

Jim would ask whether anybody felt that the Devil was troubling him, and usually a number of folks would come down from the bleachers. Jim and the other ministers would gather round the people, one by one, laying hands on their heads, praying. Some people fell down, screaming and yelling. Some began to dance and talk in tongues. It was chaos. It scared me.

Jim, to my knowledge, did not cast out demons on television in 1984.

Sometimes after Jim left the studio, Vi and Frank and Dr. Gross would lay hands on Jim and pray for him, once they'd gotten out of view of the audience.

He seemed to like it.

I also saw him cast demons out of buildings—but I'll tell you about that later.

Anyway, television evangelists, whether Pentecostal or not, generally ask for money to support their ministries—just the way your local church does. Almost, anyway.

Jim based his asking on Luke 6:38: "Give, and it shall be given unto you." In one of his inspirational works, *The Big 3 Mountain-Movers* (Logos International, 1977), he wrote: ". . . giving is . . . at the heart of Christianity. Giving is a fixed law of God. It's uniquely tied with receiving." He follows this passage with a letter from a PTL Partner, printed under the headline "Partner's $100 Gift Produces $10,000 Return."

While I was at PTL Jim was always looking for stories like that; he loved them.

The chapter in *Mountain-Movers* ends with "A Prayer for You," which ends: "From this day forth, Lord, I commit my finances to you. I put myself, my family, everything I have at your disposal. Father, I look to you for guidance in my giving. I believe you will bless my giving according to the Scriptures. I trust you, knowing you will abundantly supply all my needs. In Jesus' holy name, Amen."

Jim gave folks a lot of guidance about their giving. It was one of the keys to his theology.

The Big 3 Mountain-Movers devotes an entire chapter to giving. In it, Jim draws on an early, painful memory that would crop up again:

"During my early years as a traveling evangelist, many congregations would hold 'poundings' or canned goods showers for Tammy and me. I went to many poor churches, and some places this was the only form of offering.

"People cleaned out the junk from their closets and shelves and brought it to church for us. The gifts were unlabeled cans of food. Some of the cans were rusty and most of the food was unfit to be eaten. This was their love gift for the visiting preacher.

"The Scripture says, 'Honour the Lord with thy substance, and with the first fruits of all thine increase' (Proverbs 3:9). We are to give God our best. Then we can understandably expect the best from Him."

In 1976, the year before *The Big 3 Mountain-Movers* was published, Jim made $24,000 in salary and expenses, as reported in a recent article in *Time*.

In 1985, eight years after *Mountain-Movers'* publication, Jim was still rankled by that early memory, although he was undoubtedly receiving over $638,000 a year (roughly the compensation he received in 1983, according to a 1985 IRS report cited in *Time*).

In a 1985 sermon he said:

"You ever had a pounding? You preachers know what a pounding is? . . . Not the kind they beat you, but you know when they bring the food in. You ever have them bring in those can goods that were brown and ugly, and you couldn't figure out what was in the jar? . . . And the lids were rusted and there was dust all over it and you knew they went downstairs and it probably sat there fifty years in the cellar, and they said, 'Well, this is for the evangelist, it's good enough.' Oh, yes, nothing's too good for God's man of power, but you let them drive a Cadillac, and ohhhh. A Volkswagen's good enough.

"If you are going to win, 'good enough' is not good enough."

Jim taught that if you asked God for something in

the right way, God would give it to you. He once said, "If you pray for a camper, be sure to say what color you want, because you're going to get it." And he said, "God wants Christians to have crystal chandeliers."

He loved Matthew 18:19, and had it printed on the back of our PTL identification cards: "Again I say unto you, that if two of you shall agree on earth as touching any thing that they shall ask, it shall be done for them of my Father which is in heaven."

If I understand it correctly, the giving would somehow be a proof of the sincerity of your prayer, or help it along to unleash God's limitless goodness on you, right now, in the form of money or whatever you needed. Nobody ever seemed to think of it as trying to buy God's favor, not that I ever saw.

Tammy Faye gave an example of the power of giving in *I Gotta Be Me:* In church one day, she says, "Jim whispered to me and said, 'Honey, God has spoken to me to put in $25.' I gasped as it was all the money we had. . . . That was our grocery money. But somehow I felt good inside. We were giving it to Jesus. The service was hardly over before someone came up to us and whispered, 'Can I take you two to dinner today?' . . . . After we had eaten and were about to say thank you and good-bye, he handed us a $20 bill. And that night in church we were handed two more $20 bills. Sixty dollars the Lord had returned to us. After that, giving became easier. We always remembered what God had done with our $25."

As Jerry Falwell said in 1987, ". . . the real problem at PTL was prosperity theology. It's the same thing the Reverend Ikes and a host of television ministers preach, that God is a holy slot machine. You put in ten dollars, you get out twenty dollars, . . . especially if you give it to the person who's doing the preaching."

Hundreds of thousands of people sincerely believed they were doing God's work in sending their money to Jim.

Jim preached hard against drugs and alcohol. He was against abortion. Faithful marriage was the best way of life.

But Jim preached forgiveness rather than judgment. He wanted people to know God as a God of love, not cruel harshness.

His own early experience had been harsh. In his autobiography *Move that Mountain!* (Logos International, 1976), Jim says: "Fear had constantly pervaded my life—from the first time I saw the big 'eye' in church. It was a black and white picture of a human eye standing about three feet high on the wall of our Sunday school classroom and, to me, that eye was God Himself. And he was looking directly at me. . . . Not only was I afraid of God, even my own shadow alarmed me on occasion."

Jim wanted people to know that God was Love. Some people think he went too far, that his God was more Santa Claus than the Christian God. Some people say that the gifts of God are things like kindness, honesty, patience, love, and humility—not campers and chandeliers.

As far as I could see, Jim really believed in those campers and chandeliers as a sign of God's love.

More than most churchmen—conservative churchmen—do, he emphasized the "joy of things" that was part of the joy of God:

In that 1985 sermon called "The Greatest Thieves of the Church," he preached:

> This morning I'm going to call the final big thief, . . . the biggest thief in the church today. The thief that is killing and robbing and stealing from the church of Jesus Christ and I call him Mr. Kill Joy. Mr. Kill Joy. "Well, I don't think they should have danced in the aisles in church." "Well, you know they got a train, and that's not spiritual." . . . You don't like the train, you are really going to get upset, because in two weeks one of the most beautiful white-and-gold-horses merry-go-round is going in the middle of the park for the little kids and the grannies to ride. We have let some of the narrow-minded people dictate the whole policy of the church, and we have let them rain on our parades long enough, and I believe that it's time we get free and let Mr. Kill Joy go build his own church. . . .

He went on to say that he programmed his own ministry around the people who were determined to destroy it or make it look bad. He said that he was once afraid to get on the telephone because they were bound to give him a hard time about what he had said on the show, and he had contracted ulcers because of that. He said he overcame all this, and didn't have ulcers anymore. Because of a particular scripture in the Bible, in the book of Nehemiah, that said, "The joy of the Lord is your strength."

We are supposed to be the joyful people. We are supposed to be the happy people. So I say to you today on this first day of this Victory Week, Let the celebration begin. Let the parades go. Let the fireworks explode. Let the song be sung. Let the teachers teach. And let the people of the Lord say so." Can you say Amen? Stand up if you believe it. Give the Lord a hand. Hallelujah. God, we give you the glory, we give you the honor, we give you the victory, we love you. Hallelujah! Hallelujah! Hallelujah! The joy of the Lord is my strength.

It was a very attractive way of looking at the world. But he did preach Christian virtues, too. He urged his hearers to put their lives in God's hands.

In a sermon titled, "Who Can Be Used of God," he preached:

Somebody has to help you grow up.

But you think of what young people today are doing. So young person, don't give up. Don't stop just because someone says you can't do it. "No" means "go," remember. "No" means "go." "Can't" means "can." Just remember that when the Devil is throwing something at you. "No" means "go." The Devil doesn't know what he's talking about. He's dumb.

Tammy said the other day she was surprised that the Devil doesn't learn a new book of tricks. He uses the same thing over and over again. We ought to write a handbook, *The Devil's Stupid Tricks.*

I hope to goodness the Devil *doesn't* learn any new tricks. The tricks that have been around forever still work all too well—the tricks that human beings play on other human beings. The tricks don't change, only the players do. One of the oldest is the trick of saying "no" means "go" and "can't" means "can"—and "right" means "wrong."

If you use this trick, you can justify anything.

But it is just a trick. Using good common sense, we basically know that something that is wrong is wrong, and something that is right is right. "Right" means "right" and "wrong" means "wrong"—no matter what you hear.

Jim's sermon went on:

I want you to know, young or old, rich or poor, God wants to use you. If it hadn't been for some of the kids that nobody wanted . . . We used to call ourselves at PTL, "God's rejects." Do you remember that, Tammy? We all felt like we had been thrown out of somewhere, or given up by somebody, and we were out in the street. . . .

All that was left of . . . my vision for a television ministry was a garage full of old television monitors that we had bought from the . . . Los Angeles school system. We got these monitors for about two dollars and five dollars each, and so we bought . . . hundreds of . . . old black and white monitors. But we had a dream. . . . And you know we were just . . . a bunch of kids, the people would say. . . . And we had a vision, we had a dream. And we were probably considered crazy . . . but God said

He wanted us to build a television ministry. And it seemed like everywhere we went . . . there was those No signs coming up. Stop signs coming up. But . . . we did what we could do. . . . What a way to start a national television ministry. . . .

We bought some TV equipment that I think Noah must have used on the Ark. But we did what we could do, and we did what we had to do with, and we began to believe God. And now the largest purchaser of airtime in the world of Christianity, of air, period, worldly or any other kind, is PTL.

You say, "Oh, but Jim, I'm so weak. I'm so weak." You know what I've learned? Your weakness is probably your best asset if you will give it to God. For the word of God says, "I can do all things through Christ who strengtheneth me."

Jim had come a long way from the equipment that "Noah must have used on the Ark." In 1984 the PTL network reached over a hundred stations, and over ten million viewers. It was just enormous, and by 1987 it was even bigger. It was appearing on more than 1700 cable systems serving fourteen million subscribers. In 1987 the cameras, studios, satellite dishes, and other facilities were valued at $15 million.

The network carries shows of all religious persuasions, from Presbyterians to Baptists to Jews.

But the heart of the 1984 programming was the shows we made at PTL. And when I say "we" I mean "we." Even I took part. I played Noah in a spot once, advertising some tapes of the Bible read by Efrem Zimbalist, Jr. Jim grinned; he said it was the first time he'd seen Noah with a southern accent.

Five days a week, *The Jim Bakker Show* was shot at eleven o'clock in the morning. *The Tammy Show* began at 2:00 P.M. weekdays, until it was canceled because Tammy didn't want to do it anymore and because of the costs of producing the show. She said it was because she wanted to preach at camp meetings instead. The day she announced that to Jim, she was tearful, hyper, and on a semi-coherent talking jag.

Jim just said, "Sure, if that's what you want to do."

She never did it, though. Not while I was there.

I think she was just tired of the show. It was mostly talk and cooking—and Tammy loved to *perform*.

The Sunday worship service was televised, and so were camp meetings at 7:00 P.M. at least five nights a week. A variety of seminars were also broadcast, and telethons were staged whenever Jim thought he needed one.

I'd usually get Jim to the studio for *The Jim Bakker Show* at ten or so. He'd have the written lineup of that day's show with him; there was always a big thing about making sure that it reached the house on time.

We'd park at the back of the studio, where there was a garage, and go inside, on into his dressing room. One long wall had mirrors on it, and a shelf that served as a dressing table. There were his Certs, his Climatress hair spray, a selection of combs, nail clippers, and British Sterling—the cologne that he preferred. In front of that wall was the barber chair where he sat for makeup.

He didn't dye his hair while I was there. I have since heard that he began coloring it after I left.

His makeup girl, Penny Hollenbeck (Jim called her "Penna-LOAP," but nobody else did), was a gorgeous woman in her early twenties, a five-foot-ten blonde. She was very sweet.

Penny always put on his makeup, and usually his alone. If they really needed help with guests' makeup, Penny would help out. But Jim was her job. She was really good with the makeup, which was no surprise since they had sent her to California for a couple of weeks to train under Johnny Carson's makeup man.

Anyway, behind the barber's chair was a closet that housed seventy-five or eighty shirts and maybe forty pairs of shoes and forty or fifty suits and coats, as well as slacks and jackets and some sports clothes.

It's an IRS requirement on television performers that if they want to deduct their on-camera clothes as business expenses, then they must wear those clothes only while actually working. Because of this, Jim was supposed to change into his television clothes there in the dressing room—and change back into personal clothes before leaving. He did, about half the time.

From the dressing room you could go on into his workout room. There was a set of weights there, and a large table suitable for massages.

There was also a steam room—"weather" room might fit it better, because you could really get any type of weather in there you wanted. You could get rained on, you could get steam, you could get a sauna.

There was also a huge step-up bathtub with gold

fittings. Tammy Faye's dressing room had an entrance to the bathing area, too.

Tammy seldom used the bathing area. Jim didn't use it much, either, except for massages that he'd get one or another PTL employee to give him.

Sometimes, being outside during these sessions made me feel uneasy, but I'll tell you about that in Chapter 9.

As a matter of fact, Tammy didn't use her dressing area much. She seldom came to the studio with Jim. She'd dress at home, where she had a fabulous dressing room, then come in later.

Tammy paid a huge amount of attention to her body. She was immaculately clean, with brand-new polish on her finger- and toenails. She had her nails done in Pineville about once a week, and did them herself once or twice in between, so that the colors were coordinated to the clothes she planned to wear. Sometimes she had strange colors on her nails—lavender and gray come to mind.

She did her own makeup for the shows as well as for everyday. Her makeup was always flawless, if you can say that about Tammy's makeup. I mean that it was never smudged or messy at all, except when she'd cried and her mascara had run all down her cheeks. Considering how very heavy her makeup was, it must have taken a lot of care to have it look so fresh.

Even on the road, when Jim would sometimes come out for breakfast less than perfectly groomed, Tammy wouldn't appear at all until she was fully made up.

Her hair always looked as if she'd just that minute washed and styled it.

When Tammy was nervous, she'd cut her hair. In 1984 it was no more than two inches long, and it wasn't often you saw it.

When she was feeling bad about things—or so it seemed to those who knew her—she'd wear one of her half-dozen wigs.

Seeing Tammy with her own hair showing was a good omen to all of us—it meant she was having one of her occasional happier days.

People said she dyed her hair, but I never saw any evidence of it—no dark roots and no sudden color changes.

She always smelled wonderful. She had no one favorite scent, but switched around among a lot of expensive perfumes.

She is a little woman, under five feet tall, but she had a *very* good figure for a woman of her age. I've read that she had enlargement surgery on her breasts. They looked fine to me—she liked to emphasize them, customarily wearing clothes with deep cleavage showing. Even so, I don't think anybody would have made a fuss over the amount of cleavage if she hadn't been an evangelist's wife.

As for her style in clothes . . . Well, as a newlywed she'd admired the landlady of their first apartment. She wrote in *I Gotta Be Me:* "Lena was a real classy dame—the long cigarette, big hats, the furs, big diamonds, big car, and Estee Lauder perfumes poured all over her."

Tammy favored very long skirts, halfway between her knees and ankles. They made her look shorter, of course, so she wore teetering-high open-toed spike heels to make her look taller (I guess). The combination didn't work. It just made her look chunky, which she wasn't.

I used to think she must have had ballet training, or been to school to learn toe dancing, to be able to manage those shoes as she did. She never teetered, and she flitted around as fast as if she'd been wearing sneakers!

She wore tons of jewelry—bracelets, necklaces, earrings. I remember particularly some big old gaudy beads. She also liked gold chains, and gold pins. She even wore a gold anklet sometimes.

While Tammy was dressing and doing her makeup at home, beginning to get ready for the show, Jim would be sitting down in the barber chair in the studio dressing room.

Some time before I arrived at PTL, Jim had gone off to have a face-lift, to take up the extra skin under his chin. Is it called a chin-lift? I was told that Tammy hated that idea, that she disliked it so much that she wouldn't meet Jim at the airport when he came back.

I gathered she was afraid the chin-lift might make Jim look younger than she.

Jim's chin-lift might have been Tammy's business, in her opinion, but it didn't work the other way. More than once I heard Jim say something about her makeup, about how much of it she wore. Tammy almost always snapped back, "That's none of your business!"

And Jim would let it drop, just like that.

The chin-lift, by the way, gave Jim one unusual

characteristic—he had whisker growth behind his ears, where the skin from his chin had gone.

As Jim sat in the barber chair for Penny to work on his makeup and hair, he'd get ready for the show, deciding what he was going to do.

Dale Hill and Paul King usually came in about then. Dale and Paul were the most senior television people there while I worked at PTL.

Dale, the producer, had been with Jim for many years, starting back at *The 700 Club* where Jim worked for Pat Robertson. He was extremely professional, and very dedicated to the ministry and to Jim.

Paul was the associate producer, the guy in charge on the floor during the shows, and was also very professional. Paul had worked with Dale for a long time.

Dale and Paul would want to go over the lineup for that day, the guests that were going to be on and all that, the questions written down that he would ask—the whole thing.

Jim wasn't much on written lineups, except maybe to use the back for note-writing. He might even cancel scheduled guests—right then at the last minute—if they didn't fit in with his thinking that day. He knew in his own mind what he was going to do on the show that day. Other than some input from Dale and Paul, he'd wing the show. And he was great at it. Even when the guests had canceled out at the last minute, Jim never lost control. He'd bring in some staff to be on the show, or his kids; maybe have someone do a special song or songs with the PTL Singers and the band.

Other people were in and out. Sometimes Jeanne Johnson. Jeanne was a singer, and helped coordinate the shows. Sometimes Jim's brother Norman, who worked with the Partners, greeting them, would come in to talk.

Nobody knew what Jim was going to do until he stepped on the stage. But Jim always did. It was just so funny to me, seeing everybody whisking around trying to get everything organized—but "everything" was Jim Bakker, from start to finish. And he liked it that way.

It would be getting time for us to go out there, and Tammy would come racing in, usually at the last minute. They would get together in the back hall, a restricted area where people couldn't see them, which was often just as well.

She had a violent temper, and often arrived backstage cocked and ready to fire: screaming at Jim about something he had said or not said the night before, or about her guard or companion of the day being too slow, or her makeup didn't feel right, or the house was a wreck, or that she didn't like the guest that morning. Or she'd be carrying on about the singers, that this one wasn't good enough to be on the set, or the way that one was looking at her. Sometimes she'd be throwing a fit about four or five different things at the same time.

"My throat hurts," she'd say.

Jim would say, "You don't have to sing today if you don't feel up to it."

Generally she'd look grateful that he was paying attention to her and sympathizing with her problems. She *needed* to have people sympathize with her.

Then it was time, and the show would begin.

CHAPTER 3

Watch ye and pray, lest ye enter into temptation.

MARK 14:38

The Jim Bakker Show was usually opened by Uncle Henry Harrison. Uncle Henry was a minister who'd been with Jim for years. He'd start off: "Live from Heritage U.S.A.—It's Jim and Tammy Bakker!" And Jim and Tammy would come up through the audience, waving and smiling, and the show was on. Often they'd do the first segment right out in the audience.

Then there'd be a song, maybe; the PTL Singers or someone special, a guest.

Then Jim and Tammy would be up on the stage with the guest, or guests, who could be anybody from Dale Evans to Minnie Pearl to Pearl Bailey to Rosie Grier. I liked Dale Evans a lot. She was a real lady, with no artificial notions about special treatment due her. She was very natural.

Sometimes there was a special-interest story, somebody who was supposedly healed from some dramatic disease by faith or the power of prayer, or maybe somebody who had been in the depths of sin and had come back to God and was working special miracles, something of this nature. Or somebody who had come from rags to riches. Jim particularly wanted Christian success stories.

Jim usually tried to have something motivational on the show: somebody who could make people believe that they could do anything. This was what he tried to instill into people: "Hey," he seemed to be saying, "I did what I did. I was a toolmaker's son and look at me now."

Tammy was wonderful on camera, so caring-seeming, so nice, even on her bad days. I wondered how she could be so ugly backstage and then come out a different person. She could cry for the camera at the drop of a hat. She cried a lot on camera, but I seldom saw her cry unless she was in front of an audience.

Sometimes she sang. When it was one of her "bad throat" days, she'd tell the people they'd have to forgive her bad singing, that she wasn't feeling just right—and then she'd sing just fine. It seemed to me she was just prompting people to pay attention to her.

Her voice was beautiful, with a little of that country sound. I often thought she could have been another Loretta Lynn or Tammy Wynette.

The show gave people a lot of chances to send money. There would be "spots" for the PTL Bible, how much it was and where to send the money and how good it was; there'd be film of the Heritage Grand under construction, with the pitch on how to become a Lifetime Partner by sending in $1000 and getting free time in the hotel each year for the rest of your life. There'd be pitches for the Home for Unwed Mothers, and a lot of reminders that being a Prayer Partner was very important; that you should pledge your fifteen or twenty dollars a month and receive the literature.

I remember particularly when Jim was offering to send Christmas ornaments out to folks who sent in five-dollar or ten-dollar donations. The money came in fast. One day, on the way back to his dressing room, Jim was laughing.

He looked over at me and said, "Can you believe it, Mike? These things cost me eleven cents, and they're sending me five and ten dollars for them."

I just shook my head and smiled. These people believed in him, and he was laughing at them, making fun of them.

But I needed the job, and I knew if I made any objection I'd be out real quick. I wasn't proud of it.

That exchange was kind of important, I think. After that Jim didn't seem to care what he said in front of me. I guess he thought we saw things the same way. I think, too, that this was when I realized that I didn't see things his way nearly so much as I had believed.

Jim could be cruel in public, too, about people who came to visit Heritage U.S.A. In a 1985 sermon, he preached:

A person whose own heart is evil and untrusting finds evil in everything. You know I had people tell me that they went to the Heritage Grand, you will all look at this today now. But they went at the canopy outside of the Heritage Grand where you drive up. I just nicely got it finished and it circulated throughout my staff that there was Devil faces in the aluminum, or the tin ceilings underneath the canopy. I went out there, and I've got an imagination. I mean I've got an imagination. I couldn't find an angel. I couldn't find a Devil. I couldn't find a car. I couldn't find a cow. I couldn't find a horse. All I saw was the pattern of the tin ceiling. Somebody had wicked imaginations and was spreading it all over that there were demon pictures underneath the canopy of the Heritage Grand. [That's evil seeing evil instead of pure seeing goodness in everything they can possibly find.] And I am tired of those people running our churches, running our denominations, and running our movements. Running all that we do, and we listen to that trash.

But Jim *taught* people to look for the Devil and his works!

To get back to Jim's show: in addition to the other "commercials," there was always the message that to give to PTL would make you able to do anything you wanted.

Sometimes the selling time took up almost *all* of the show, but other days hardly any time at all was spent asking for money. If I had to guess an average, I'd say fifteen minutes in the hour—about like commercial television. The amount of time spent asking for money depended entirely on Jim's moods and needs. And if times got rocky, if the money was tight, he'd do a telethon. Then it was just about all commercials.

After the show Jim would stay and visit with the audience, sometimes for five minutes, sometimes for an hour and a half. It was just according to the kind of response he got from the crowd. Usually he'd stand right at the foot of the bleachers, but keeping his distance from the people.

It was after a telethon one night that the guy made the run at Jim.

Usually, Security tried to pay attention to people as they were coming in, and removed people that looked or acted as if they had emotional or mental problems, people who looked as if they would cause a disturbance. Security also relied on the ushers who seated people to help out, and they did. We might go for days without a problem, then we might have problems daily. It seemed to run in irregular cycles.

On this particular day, I'd picked one man out at the beginning of the show. I always scanned the audience looking for fanatics—I use the term loosely, I suppose. I mean I looked for people who looked like trouble.

This guy was seated halfway up the audience. He was a big man in his late thirties, around six-foot-five—five inches taller than I am. I noticed he couldn't be still, but was mumbling to himself and standing up and sitting down, standing up, sitting back down. I eased through the audience and spread the word to all the guards—we usually had four to six in the studio. They all kind of watched the guy. He just didn't seem right.

As the show continued, he got to be a little more

than I could take, jumping up and down, doing a little hollering, "Hallelujah" and "Praise God." So I went up in the audience behind him and put my hand on his shoulder. It was dripping wet with sweat.

"Are you okay?" I asked.

"I'm fine, I'm fine. I just feel the Spirit moving in me." He was wild-eyed.

"Are you sure you are okay?" I could feel his shoulder trembling.

He told me again he was fine.

I thought, Let's go ahead and get him out of here.

But I didn't want to disrupt the show and make the other people in the audience uneasy, so I just whispered to him, "Well, just take it easy, the show is almost over, just take it easy and everything will be all right." I made sure the other guards were still keeping an eye on him and went back down to be near Jim.

Jim had ended the show, and had stepped down onto the forty-foot-wide strip of smooth concrete between the set and the bleachers. I looked over at him, and the next thing I knew I caught this blur coming out of the stands, and this guy was just running, screaming at the top of his lungs, and he was reaching into his pocket. I saw him trying to get something out and it was black. And the first thing I thought was that this guy has got a gun and he's going to get to Jim. He was screaming "Bakker! Bakker! Bakker!"

Now, I had a gun, a .38 revolver; I carried a gun at all times, except on commercial airliners, either in a holster or in my briefcase. But working in law enforcement taught me never to draw a gun unless I intended to use it, and I just couldn't see using a gun in there with all the people. If he did have a gun, I figured the safest thing I could do was to get to that gun before it was used.

I was twenty or thirty feet behind Jim, but by the time the guy reached that cement floor, I had up a full head of steam and I hit him head-on. I tried to hit him hard enough to crush him in his footsteps. I had already sized this man up, and I knew it would take a terrific physical blow to stop him. I managed to send his feet right up in the air. I guess playing football teaches you how to tackle.

I had him down, but he was still screaming and trying to get his hand in his pocket, and I was afraid it was a gun and he was going crazy. I was frantic to get his arm pinned down. As I succeeded, some of the other guards arrived to help me. They got him up and took him out of there.

The pain was really setting in. I'd had three operations on my left knee, thanks to playing football in the Marines, and that knee had hit the concrete *hard.* So had the other one, for that matter. And my head was splitting.

Jim hadn't moved. He was still standing in the same spot, just a few feet away. Now, without missing a breath, he told the audience: "Ladies and gentlemen, I apologize for this little incident. Sometimes my bodyguard thinks somebody is trying to harm me and he gets a little overreactive."

He had complete control of the audience, and none of them even moved. I mean, it was as if we'd staged the incident. Everyone went on listening to Jim. It just goes to show how much power he had over people.

It sure didn't feel like much thanks to me, what he'd said. But after all, it was my job. I was just doing it. I guess he didn't want to upset anybody.

I went on out to the back room and talked to the guy a little bit. The black thing in his pocket was a plastic change purse. We never found out what he wanted to do with it. He didn't know, either. He just wanted to get to Bakker.

We didn't have any grounds to hold him on, so we took his name and address and escorted him out the front gate.

Jim never did thank me exactly, but later, in the car with Tammy Faye, Jim told her, "If I've ever been afraid of someone harming me, I have to say this, as long as I am with Mike I'll never worry about that again."

It was true, he didn't have to. Now he knew that I'd die for him if I had to. That's the way I saw my job. I'd taken it on, and I'd do it to the best of my ability. If it meant getting harmed or even killed, that was just what would have to happen.

Tammy Faye seemed to have a lot more to do with me after that. Until then I'd seen her temper tantrums and her bad side almost exclusively, although I'd had a few glimpses of her more pleasant side.

One morning early on, as I was out in the car waiting for Jim at the house, Tammy had come flying up the steps—it was very unusual for her to leave the house first; I don't remember why it happened that day—and came over to the car.

"You must be Mike," she said, with a big, warm smile. "Good morning. How are you today?"

I said fine, and good morning, and then she was

zipping over to her own car, where Richard Dortch's daughter, Deanna Dortch Collins, was waiting for her. Tammy got in, in the driver's seat. She *loved* to drive.

She'd smelled *goood,* and was perfectly groomed, and what had impressed me was how quickly she moved.

She'd been naturally pleasant and warm, too.

In the months between, I'd seen much more of the hellcat, not that she was yelling at me, just that I was in the neighborhood. On her bad days, of which there were so many, there'd be no "Good morning." She was just so wrapped up in her own gripes.

Now, after the guy's run at Jim, she seemed to notice me more fully as a human being. She said, "Good morning" or "Hi, Mike," more regularly, and would sometimes stop to exchange a couple of sentences with me. She was a "touchy" person, and would reach out to pat my arm while we talked.

It seemed like she really began to trust me.

Jim appeared to have no concern about his own life. He really didn't seem to be afraid. He was the opposite about Tammy and the kids, though, asking lots of questions about their protection and safety. He really worried about them a lot; about himself, not at all.

As far as Tammy Faye went, Jim wasn't just concerned for her personal safety.

He was super-jealous of Tammy. *Super.*

In the afternoons he'd check several times through the Security system: where was she? who was with her?

We had trouble keeping people with Tammy Faye

that year. They weren't always security guards; sometimes they were simply female companions. If Tammy Faye didn't care for somebody, or if she couldn't get along with him, or thought he couldn't get along with her, she wouldn't allow that person around her. It didn't have to be a good reason, or even a real reason, that I saw. With a lot of things she thought people had done—things that made her decide she didn't want them around—it was just something she had imagined. This sort of thing could happen not only with security guards and female companions, but also with other people.

About the people who were allowed around her, about most things, Tammy Faye almost always got her own way. She was like a little kid in some ways. She didn't like this. She didn't like that. She didn't like certain people. She was always telling Jim what people had said. I just have to say she did a lot of whining.

One of her companions, for a while, was Deanna Dortch Collins, but Deanna couldn't suit Tammy as a daily companion. She liked Deanna; their temperaments were just different. Tammy liked to move fast, and she'd get impatient with Deanna's more normal speed.

Deanna was miserable with Tammy, although she tried hard. Deanna was a tenderhearted person.

Deanna was later relieved of her duty of being with Tammy on a daily basis, and I was happy for her that she was.

We went through several companions while I was there.

One day early on, Tammy Faye came up to me

at the studio and asked me to drive her home to Tega Cay.

I agreed.

She was by herself.

I don't remember exactly what we talked about on the way home, but I do remember very vividly that she opened up to me. She kind of turned in the passenger seat, and she was talking to me warmly and in a personal way.

It wasn't like taking your boss's wife home.

It was more like taking a first date home, to tell you the truth.

She had the same kind of perky, silly, vulnerable charm a teenage girl does. She really was cute, in that same teenage way. And she really was vulnerable.

All in all, Tammy was just as sexy as could be.

I didn't take her hand. But I was very conscious of her as a woman.

There was nothing wrong with her—her teeth were good, her feet were pretty, her legs were good, her skin looked like satin, and she had the look of a real woman.

And her figure was good.

She looked at least ten years younger than her age.

Look at her pictures again, subtract the makeup and the shoulder pads, and the chunky clothes she likes to wear . . .

You'll see a really pretty woman. Very petite—but she has it all.

I tried to dismiss my misgivings from my mind, and had made some progress towards doing so when David Taggart came up to me a day or two later.

"Did you take Tammy Faye home by herself?" he asked me, as if he was hoping I'd say no.

"Sure," I said.

"Don't ever do that again."

"What?" I exploded guiltily. Had Jim been reading my mind?

"And make sure no male guard is ever alone with her. Especially you." He sounded emphatic.

"What are you talking about? That's ridiculous!"

"It's his order," David said.

I walked away, shaking my head for David's benefit.

Once I was alone I thought about it.

I'd heard from a third person that Tammy had earlier said I was "good-looking," and I wondered if Jim had heard that opinion.

Also, my ride home with Tammy had caused me to think about her. I had noticed even before that incident how she seemed to want and need a lot of reassurance, little compliments when she looked pretty, little attentions that showed she mattered, such as being sure to help her into and out of the car.

It had seemed to me that she often took backseat in this ministry, and was considered to tag along behind Jim.

It's true that she took no part in the business of the ministry, but she was important to the Partners. They'd ask for her when they didn't see her. And when she missed a show, a lot of get-well cards would pour in.

I think the Partners saw beyond the thick makeup and the chunky clothes to the vulnerable woman. I know I did. She seemed to me a woman who needed a friend, and I made up my mind to try and be a friend to her.

I wondered if Jim had already noticed that.

I kept Jim's order in mind for the rest of my time at PTL.

It wasn't just that it was an order. It was also because I didn't trust myself around her. I was afraid I might do or say something I might later regret. I knew that Jim's eye was always on her, and I knew I'd be fired if he saw as much as an admiring look on my face.

From then on, if I was alone in a room and she walked in, I'd get out of that room as fast as I could. Still, I tried to let Tammy know by my public actions that she had a friend who cared about her comfort and safety.

A lot of people thought Jim was unreasonably jealous of Tammy, the way he was always wanting to know where she was and who was with her, making sure a woman he trusted was with her, checking up on her a half-dozen times a day. But it was true that an aura of sexiness came off her.

She liked sex and didn't care who knew it. She could always find a sexy double meaning in an innocent remark.

Once, when I was taking them home very late, she offered me the guest bedroom. I said, "No thanks, I'm just going to go home and go to bed." She flashed back, "Who're you going to bed with, Mike?"

She'd often say, "Sex with Jim is always good," and "If I can only get Jim in bed I can have anything I want," and they certainly spent a *lot* of time in the bedroom, although they didn't impress me as running in there to make love. But the way they were, I did think his jealousy unreasonable—until I heard the stories that were told me by PTL people about Tammy's affairs of the heart.

In 1980 Tammy Faye had an affair of the heart with Christian country singer/composer Gary Paxton, I was told. Gary and his wife Karen had known the Bakkers for several years, and the Paxtons appeared regularly on Jim and Tammy's show. Gary had produced some of Tammy's records, too. "When the closeness between the two became obvious," *People* magazine wrote in 1987, "Karen divorced her husband. She believes, however, that the Tammy-Paxton relationship was not consummated." Tammy and Gary also say it was "an innocent crush," according to *People*.

Jim put a stop to it by severing Paxton-PTL connections.

I was told Tammy had been with Jim in December 1980 in Clearwater Beach, Florida, on the day John Wesley Fletcher introduced Jim to Miss Jessica Hahn.

Fletcher was an Assemblies of God minister who had visited at PTL, and who was later defrocked—*dismissed* is the word the Assemblies use—for unacceptable conduct.

Tammy was out shopping that afternoon.

The kids were down by the pool. A Bakker friend was minding them—a friend who, I was told, was one of the PTL wife-swappers.

After Florida, the Bakkers went to Hawaii. That's when Tammy left him and went to California to live, renting an apartment in the Los Angeles area.

Over the preceding year, I was told, Tammy had

developed a growing closeness to Thurlow Spurr, the well-liked music director of PTL. I was told that Tammy says she called Thurlow from California and told him not to leave his wife and join her there.

I was also told that Tammy said they were never actually lovers.

She went to work in a hospital during this time, I was told.

Tammy stayed away for three months.

Well, after Tammy left, the story went on, Jim told three or four people at PTL what had happened in Florida: that he'd had a twenty-minute sexual encounter with Hahn that had not included intercourse. He felt extremely remorseful and guilty; he said he'd just wanted to make Tammy jealous. One PTL executive, a woman, advised him that he was on the right track; that he ought to make her as jealous as he could. "No," Jim responded (or so I was told), "it's wrong. There has to be another way to get her back."

Jim was terribly unhappy. Another PTL executive told me he sometimes stayed with Jim all night, really afraid that Jim might commit suicide. Jim was desperate to get her back.

Somehow Jim persuaded Tammy to attend a marriage seminar with him in Palmdale, California. There, Jim met with Fred Gross, in 1984 a member of PTL's Marriage Workshop team. In March 1987, Dr. Gross told the Associated Press that in 1981 Jim had been "racked with pain and guilt from the head to his toes."

In Palmdale, Jim and Tammy also met Vi Azvedo. Jim felt that it was Vi who put his marriage back together, and his gratitude and loyalty to her were real.

Tammy's tension and mood swings in 1983–84 may have been partly the result of being a prisoner of jealousy—it's hard to live with deep distrust—although, of course, her problems with Valium were undoubtedly mainly to blame.

Tammy got a little uneasy about only one woman, as far as I could see. She was very cool, as if a little jealous, to lovely young Penny Hollenbeck, Jim's makeup girl. But I never saw Jim make any maneuvers toward Penny. He liked her, that was all.

I really sensed that Tammy Faye felt something was wrong with their marriage, but she had nothing to blame it on other than another woman—and Penny was the only one she had to blame it on.

As for Jim, in the entire year I spent with him, I never saw him look at Penny or any other woman with desire, never even heard him say so much as "There's a good-looking woman."

CHAPTER 4

Ye are the light of the world. A city that is set on an hill cannot be hid.

MATTHEW 5:14

The shows were a great part of the religious life at PTL, but they weren't all of it. There was religion everywhere I looked.

Sunday services were held in the Barn, which was, in fact, the Heritage Village Church. The majority of the time, Jim conducted the services. Sunday morning was my favorite time with him. He loved to preach, and he was almost always in a very happy mood on the way over to the church, joking and smiling. On Sunday mornings it was as if television didn't exist.

Tammy usually came to church separately—she really didn't seem anxious to be in Jim's company most of the time—and the first-shift guards usually took the kids over earlier for Sunday school.

Services usually began with the audience singing along with one or another leader. Then the audience would break up into small four- or five-person prayer groups, each group deciding what special request to pray for. In one group it might be a member's sick mother; in another, a member's troubled child.

During the opening song, there'd often be speaking in tongues, and people almost always waved their hands in the air.

Vi told me once I should raise my hands, too; that Jim had noticed I wasn't doing it; but I ignored her. I wasn't going to act a part I didn't believe in. And Jim never said anything to me about it. I knew it wasn't like him to try to give orders about the way another person believed.

Tammy often spoke in tongues during the service, but I never saw Jim do it.

After prayer there'd be a song by the PTL Singers. And they'd pass the plate.

Then Jim would preach his sermon. He was the best preacher I have ever heard. He had the feel for the crowd and the feel for the people. Maybe he was only five-foot-six, but put him at that podium and he was six-five. He was a wonderful salesman, you might say. They say the key to selling is to persuade people to think the way you think, and he could do that brilliantly.

I fought being persuaded. I didn't want to get engulfed in his world like other people I saw around him that had done so. I had a natural tendency to fight it off. But a lot of times, I would find myself almost in a trance listening to him.

In most Christian churches, the service sort of takes off from a special point in the Christian year, so that the calendar moves through Christ's time in the desert to Easter to Pentecost, and so on. But Heritage

Village Church services didn't do that. They were more free-form, you might say.

The Upper Room, named and carefully modeled after the location where Jesus and the disciples had the Last Supper, was the twenty-four-hour-a-day prayer center, which had been dedicated in 1982.

Jim had said at its dedication: "In these last days, the Upper Room will be a place where united prayer will ascend to God twenty-four hours a day on behalf of His people so that we too may be empowered to live triumphant, overcoming lives, and to preach the Gospel to the ends of the earth."

The "last days" Jim mentioned are the last days before the Second Coming of Christ. Many people believe that Christ is going to return in the year 2000, and on Christian television you can hear preachers saying all the prophecies of the Book of Revelation are being fulfilled.

The same kind of thing happened just before the year 1000—people started believing Christ was going to come back then. A lot of people took to religion then, too, and gave most of what they had to the church.

Myself, I think I'll wait and see.

Anyway, Jim credited the Upper Room, in public, with the survival of PTL. According to *Jim and Tammy Bakker Present the Ministries of Heritage Village Church* (Heritage Village Church Missionary Fellowship, Inc. 1986), Jim said God spoke to him and told him to build an Upper Room of intercessory prayer.

" *'If you will build this for me,'* said the Lord, *'then I will save your ministry.'* "

Upstairs was one big room, with long tables and benches, where people could pray or talk or attend seminars, and a number of small rooms where small groups or individuals could pray, each furnished with a Bible, and a table and chair.

Downstairs was a phone bank, staffed mostly by volunteers, taking calls from the people who wanted to be prayed for.

More than once Vi Azvedo came begging me to volunteer, because they were shorthanded.

No way, I told her. I've always felt I more needed somebody to pray for me, rather than being fit to pray for other people. I know I'm a sinner. By the way I was brought up in religion, I'm going to go to hell, because I drink beer and smoke cigarettes, curse a little bit, and chase women.

I wouldn't volunteer for the prayer phones, but a lot of people did. They did have those phones covered twenty-four hours a day.

And they did anoint the prayer requests, just as PTL said they would. Not the phone calls, of course, but the notes that the volunteers took, and the letters that came in asking for prayer.

Usually they used olive oil, just putting a drop or two on each letter. I know anointing of *people* is biblical, but I don't remember the Book talking about anointing other things. I never did understand that.

Anyway, once the General Store, which was the store on the Heritage grounds, ran out of olive oil. Vi had asked me to pick some up.

I went back, to find out what to do.

"Just bring us some Wesson Oil," Vi said.

So I did. I never heard whether it worked any better or worse.

People prayed all over PTL whenever and wherever they felt like it. It made driving on the twisty, narrow road really hazardous. A couple might be crossing the road when one of them said, "Let's pray" and they'd both close their eyes and stand there in the middle of the road praying. You had to be alert behind the wheel. Sometimes it was whole groups of them, children and all, hands waving in the air, speaking in tongues.

If you wanted somebody to pray with you, you didn't have to go looking for a minister at PTL. The Circuit Ridin' Preacher would come to you. The Circuit Ridin' Preacher was a guy named Robert Vaughan. He was all tricked out like a Western preacher—black suit, string tie, hat—and he rode his horse, Coke, through the campgrounds daily in the summer. He'd stop and tie his horse to the bumper of your camper, and come and visit if you wanted him to.

He was also, in the summer of 1984, resident minister for all those living on the PTL grounds. He baptized Partners, conducted seminars, made hospital calls, and led a Bible study for folks who lived in Dogwood Hills.

That year there were at least fifteen to twenty PTL pastors. There were daily Bible study groups, and prayer groups too. You could spend all day, and up to midnight, studying and praying if you wanted to.

The whole of Heritage U.S.A. was like a big church all day every day. Sometimes I thought it was more religion than even Jim wanted.

The Partners were so *dedicated.* They really believed. Like gamblers in Las Vegas looking for a place to spend their money, the Partners were looking for a place to pray . . . looking for . . . hungry for . . . Whatever it was, they were hungry for it. A Christian life, I guess.

It's important to remember that PTL was not just a theme park, or a television studio, or a money-collection point, or a religious organization.

It was a little town, and Jim envisioned it from the beginning as "designed to equip believers for total Christian living."

People *lived* at Heritage U.S.A.—about six hundred when I started, eight hundred or more when I left. They were mostly, if not all, retirees and PTL employees. I didn't know anybody who lived there and commuted into Charlotte, except for a few men and women married to PTL employees.

They shopped at the General Store, which Jim liked to visit personally, making sure that the shelves were in order, that all the stock was there that should be. The markups were not too bad—about what you'd find in a convenience store. It was more like a convenience store than a supermarket. It had packaged meats but no butcher, for instance. For basic grocery shopping people would go off grounds to Pineville, N.C. (three or four miles) or to Fort Mill, S.C. (about five miles). The General Store differed from the usual convenience store in one important way—it had a big gift department selling jewelry, as well as PTL books, records, and tapes. Jim's and Tammy's books and records were given prominent display.

There was a bank on the property—Home Federal Savings and Loan, which financed most if not all of the house and condo sales. (PTL didn't hold mortgages.) In 1984 Home Federal had a trailer out there, but once the Heritage Grand opened they moved into it.

There was a Christian school, the Heritage Village Church Academy, that covered all grades from kindergarten to twelfth grade. There were about a hundred kids in it. The school was in the Total Learning Center. Tammy Sue and Jamie Charles went there.

The Total Learning Center also held the Heritage Village School of Evangelism and Communications, where people could learn about the ins and outs of television, evangelism, and related topics.

Jim wanted to build a medical facility there, for emergency care. In 1984, the closest doctor was in Pineville or Fort Mill.

There was a whole little town of people at PTL, people who wanted to live the dream full-time, I guess.

Jim had a dream of making the town self-sufficient, and wanted it to grow to 50,000 people. He felt that the town should be important in the area. He wanted the local politicians to pay more attention to him than they did. He felt the mayors of Charlotte and Fort Mill should be seeking his favor. He looked forward to the day when he'd have enough residents at Heritage U.S.A. to swing an election. A York County sheriff's election was coming up while I was there, and I remember he wanted the county to come out and register everybody. I don't think it happened.

Jim liked Reagan, with his support of traditional

family values, and Reagan had said nice things about the network of PTL Centers which distributed food and clothing to the needy. But Jim wasn't a die-hard Republican. He also liked Jimmy Carter a lot, because he'd been on Air Force One with Jimmy, prayed with him, and laid hands on him. He liked to mention this, and his other meetings with prominent politicians, to stress the importance of religion in America.

Jim wasn't just impatient with employees about getting things done, but seemed to think he could get political decisions made with a snap of his fingers. He felt he was a force to be reckoned with. One day he told me he wanted the speed limit lowered from 55 to 45 on the road past the gate, because people should have to go slow and look. He told me to call a member of the board of commissioners, and get the change that afternoon.

I let it die. He was so used to getting instant results; but I knew this one would never work.

He never brought it up again.

The building of Heritage U.S.A. was in top gear in 1984. Roe Messner's firm, Commercial Builders of Kansas, was the chief builder. The firm filed suit in 1987 for fourteen million dollars, and is the largest unsecured creditor listed in the bankruptcy proceedings. The $14 million, Messner said, was owed him on the Heritage Towers and other buildings—but I'm getting ahead of myself.

First came the Heritage Grand Hotel. The idea was elaborate. As you stood with your back to the lake, the first section on the left would be a large rectangular section of hotel rooms built around an open center. Next to it would be the atrium, a large roofed space including an indoor swimming pool, with skylights overhead. To the right of the atrium would be another section of rooms—some running along the lake, and some running along the parking lot behind. Down the middle of this section would run the roofed street of shops—Main Street, U.S.A.—which would lead to the 650-seat Crystal Palace Cafeteria.

Beyond the cafeteria would be the final section of the Grand . . . or of the Partner Center (both names were used). The final section would be the Hall of Agreement auditorium.

Why such an elaborate hotel?

Nothing was too good for God's people. As *Heritage Village Church* put it, "Jim knew that drab, outmoded campgrounds would no longer appeal to Christians who were taking their vacations in clean, modern, well-planned but secular theme parks and recreation centers. God impressed on Jim . . . the need to carry the spirit of the camp-meeting movement into the twenty-first century."

Jim had had the idea for the hotel for a while, but he couldn't figure out the financing. He couldn't get banks to back him, despite giving their people guided tours and the whole pitch. This made him mad, and he looked forward to the day when he could say, "I told you so."

Jim was building the first model one-family detached house at Mulberry Village; while I was there two more models, and ten additional houses, were completed. Twenty or thirty more were started. Jim went by to see that first model almost daily.

As we pulled up, he'd grab the radio and tell V. J. Sherk, the vice-president who dealt with real estate, about the landscaping: "The shrubs are to be here and here. I want the fence to run from there to there."

He was very detail-oriented. I got so good at seeing what he was seeing that I'd know what he was going to yell about. It amazed me that others who had been around him longer than I could not see this.

As the work went on, he'd hurry inside, saying, "The couch should go on this wall. This area needs some things on the wall, some pictures of country settings."

And when the model was nearing completion, "This *is* a *cute* little doll's house! I've *got* to bring Tammy down to see this!"

Getting Tammy Faye to visit any of his projects was usually as difficult as dragging a camel through a desert, but this time she was in a good mood and she came. She also found it "cute."

When Tammy was having a good day, she was really likable. The good days came about once a week, no more, but then I'd see little glimpses of a warm, caring person.

She'd say hello to people, ask how they were, and seem interested in the answers. She seemed like a real woman then.

She was really nice, when she was nice at all, and she was fun to be around. She had a shrill, earsplitting laugh—an awful laugh—but she had a pleasant warm giggle, and I heard a lot of them on good days.

She loved to joke, and she was very funny, although a lot of her jokes had a mean edge to them.

I remember her being very funny about other ministers' wives—but the jokes, though funny, struck me as not being very kind.

She'd be agreeable on her good days, too. Usually she'd find something to object to in whatever it was Jim wanted to do, but there were her sweet days when the restaurant he wanted to go to suited her fine, when she seemed to listen to him, when she would come and look at projects he wanted to show her.

As well as Mulberry Village, Jim was building two-story townhouse apartments behind Dogwood Hills, and during 1984 would add about 150 units to the hundred or so already existing at Dogwood Hills.

He said, both in private and on television, that he had 5,000 people on the waiting list of apartments.

The first five villas went up at Wood Ridge, plus 200 to 300 apartments at the Meadows, out of the 500 that were planned. He was building the Lakeside Lodges condominiums on Lake Heritage. Eighteen units were complete when I came, eighteen more were being built while I was there. Also under construction was a huge clubhouse with a sunken fireplace—called Lakeside Activity Lodge—for the lodge residents to use.

The Lakeside Lodges were planned for sale on a time-sharing basis, at $10,000 for a week a year, but PTL wasn't supposed to use the term *time-sharing* on the air. I don't know whether it was illegal or against FCC regulations, or what, but it was a definite "no-no." Well, Jim would forget, and say "time-sharing."

David Taggart, his personal assistant, would turn

to me and groan, "I can't *believe* he's doing it again!" Then he'd get to Jim after the show, and tell him he really couldn't do it again.

David was always reminding Jim of things he should or shouldn't do on television, legal things. David talked to the attorneys in more detail than Jim did, and he seemed to take his responsibility to keep Jim informed very seriously.

At least once Jim blew up. "The FCC is trying to control everything I do! It's just another example of the Devil and his organization trying to destroy something good!" Jim customarily thought this way. Whatever he did was right; if you didn't agree, you were siding with the Devil.

It made me angry to hear him refer to our government as the Devil. We all dislike the IRS, but no way is it the Devil. It's part of this country, and I love this country.

Even local public bodies could come in for being called the Devil. In his book *Survival,* Jim strongly implies that Satan is at work when a church is refused a driveway permit. Or a sewer permit.

Jim hated hearing about rules he had to obey. He was so convinced his way was right.

A few days later Jim would forget, and say "time-sharing" again—and poor David would repeat the warning. "Yeah, yeah, I know," Jim would say, kind of waving him off.

This repeated lapse made David furious, and he'd curse Jim's stupidity and boldness. He didn't do it in front of Jim, of course, but he didn't seem to mind much who else heard.

The building projects I've told you about weren't

the only ones. Jim bought and installed a second water tower; he relandscaped North Lost Lake campground, installing concrete slabs for campers to park on. He built three unusual single-family houses behind the Youth Center. They were round, and each was raised some ten feet off the ground on a single pedestal. The Welcome Center, "the lobby of PTL," Jim called it, was under construction too.

Plans were announced for "truly unique homes . . . beginning at 2000 square feet" at Lake Park Place. They came to nothing that year.

But on top of all these projects, Jim was determined to make the Heritage Grand Hotel work. There was just one problem.

CHAPTER 5

Seest thou these great buildings?
MARK 13:2

The problem Jim was facing was how to pay for the Heritage Grand.

In early to mid-December, people started opening up more and more to me, telling me how things worked at PTL. One senior employee told me he'd had an idea for the financing. The hotel was supposed to cost $25,000,000 at the time; that was the projected cost. So, he said that he was going to suggest to Jim that what they ought to do was go on the air and ask 25,000 people to donate $1000 each, and what they would do is let them stay in the hotel for a day or two a year for the rest of their lives.

About a week later, Jim told me in the car that God had told him that the way they were going to pay for the hotel was that 25,000 people would donate $1000 each and the hotel would be paid off in cash. God? I thought to myself. Well, maybe he meant God had given the idea to the guy who had talked to me.

A couple of days later, after a big meeting of the executives where Jim presented "his" plan, he went on the air and started asking for the money. He called the donors Lifetime Partners.

The money started coming in.

About the first of January, we had the ground-breaking ceremony at the hotel site. All the Board of Directors were there, including Efrem Zimbalist, Jr., Aimee Cortese, and Richard Dortch—who would join PTL as the number-two man within the month.

All the PTL cameras were out there too, so they could air the ceremony. All the higher-ups had shovels. There was ribbon-cutting. It was a big event.

Jim had promised people it would be ready for the Fourth of July; but almost immediately after the ground-breaking, wet weather set in and the work slowed to a crawl. It was the Devil's work, that rain, Jim said; but then everything that interfered with his plans was liable to be called the Devil.

The builder, Roe Messner, was said to own as much as a city block out in Wichita. His firm, Commercial Builders, was said to have built some eight hundred or nine hundred churches in forty-seven states; in 1984 he was chief builder for PTL.

Roe was a well-built man in his forties, about five-foot-ten. He was a scratch golfer, and we talked often about having a game together, but we never did. He was as cool as a cucumber, and knew how to stay calm when Jim was keyed up.

Well, Jim fussed and fumed at the rain, but he wouldn't let rain or mud get in his way. Every day he'd go out to see what was happening, or to show some visitor what the progress was.

I took to carrying a pair of galoshes in the trunk of the car, and then more pairs, until I had about ten pairs in there, and towels too, to wipe the mud off Jim and the visitors he'd take to see the construction. I carried a raincoat for Jim, too. Nobody ever asked me to carry these things, but I learned to anticipate.

Jim liked to have people anticipate what he wanted done. If you could stay three or four moves ahead of him, that was fine; if you didn't, it was as if you had disappointed him, and he could get mean then.

I got pretty good at this, enough that I could usually even tell when he was hungry or thirsty without his saying a word. If we were inside, I would get a glass of water and take it to him, and he'd nonchalantly reach out and take it without even stopping his meeting. Outdoors, if it was hot, I'd take him a cold soft drink and hold it where he could see it, and he would take it the same way, without even stopping talking.

He liked fruit, especially bananas, so I kept a bag of fruit in an ice chest in the trunk of the car, too. When I sensed that he was hungry, I'd take him a piece of fruit; he would take it, and I'd step back, just like that.

It was always the same, whether he was meeting with some of the vice-presidents or some visiting evangelist, even the big names, like Oral Roberts. They'd always stop what they were saying and stare as if they couldn't figure out how I knew what he wanted. Jim never even slowed down, though. It was what he expected. He never said "Thank you," either. Still, he always found some way to let me know he appreciated it.

One day when we were out at the Heritage Grand construction site, Jim was walking without looking where he was going, concentrating on something in the distance, as he usually did, and he stepped spang in a big puddle. He was instantly up halfway to his knees. He gave a yelp, and sat down, *plop!* I could hardly keep a straight face. He was always so neat and clean, almost prissily so, and here he was in the mud, covered with it! He was stuck in it. I had to pull him out, finally. I managed to keep from laughing, and once he'd figured out that he wasn't hurt, he laughed, embarrassed.

After the New Year, the weather cleared up, and Jim was in a lather. He'd promised the hotel for July 4, so he had less than six months to complete the 500-room hotel. He got Roe to put on twenty-four-hour shifts. There were thousands of people there trying to build the thing; they were so desperate for help they were pulling in just anybody they could get their hands on who could do the job.

I began to wonder about theft: what with the extraordinary speed Jim was demanding on this massive project, there was no way to control all the building supplies being brought in. And I started feeling uneasy about taking Jim to the site. I was afraid some bad actor would push him off a wall or drop something on him. But the people working there just gawked at him, hundreds of them. You know, like he was some kind of god.

Later Roe insisted on slowing down the work, because he wasn't getting paid, and that's when Jim did something I still can't forgive him for. But that's a story for later.

Jim involved himself in every detail of the building, and made changes in the plans on an almost daily basis, new ideas that came to him. I couldn't believe how calmly Roe took these alterations. I guess his expertise helped him, there. Jim had to have things just exactly the way he wanted them, even if that way changed from day to day. The street of shops in the hotel—he must have made Roe tear it up two or three times to get it right.

But when Jim got keyed up, Roe didn't.

Sometimes I fibbed to protect Roe from Jim's unreasonable demands, although Roe didn't ask me to. He wasn't there every day for all those months, of course. Sometimes Jim would say, "Find Roe for me! Get him back here!"

I'd know Roe was out on the golf course, or in Florida, taking a break, but I'd tell Jim he was away on business. Jim often forgot that people had lives outside of PTL.

Well, in the early spring Jim had a telethon just for the Heritage Grand. The success of that telethon may have been the beginning of the end for Jim at PTL.

The studio was set up with Jim's usual stage, plus four or five little ones set up in hallways nearby, decorated to represent various areas of the country. There was a "Northeast" stage, for instance, with New England pictures and decor; the staffers there were chosen for their New England accents and they were carefully dressed in wintery clothes. The "South" stage looked southern, and the people had southern accents, and so on. It was all carefully designed to suggest that the people were actually in whatever area it was.

When staffers took a pledge, they would write it out, perhaps with the reason the pledge was being made—perhaps the individual had bought one partnership the week before, then had suddenly come into a windfall.

Behind the scenes, a running total of success stories and big pledges was kept. Jim would check, then say, "Let's visit the Northeast, to see how things are going." And then Jim would go to whatever stage had the greatest success stories.

The telethon showed film of the hotel that was made fresh each day. It was presented in a way to suggest that reporters from *your* area were down there following the building of the hotel.

It was a neat selling idea. It sure kept the phones ringing.

Roe Messner made appearances on the telethon, too, talking about the progress of construction. That added credibility and helped sales.

I knew Jim and Dortch were keeping careful count of the number of Partnerships sold. Richard Dortch was counting them personally. Some of the pledges were no good—bad credit cards, or people just wouldn't send the money. At first I was told they were just overselling enough to cover those "bad" pledges. It was also true that the cost of the hotel was mounting daily.

But Jim was really overselling the hotel, bad pledges or no, and he knew he was. The two weeks of the telethon really poured the money in. And after that, he continued selling Partnerships on the daily show. Nobody important seemed to care, as far as I could see.

Jim told David in my presence that it was an easy way to raise money—it seemed never-ending.

It seemed much easier than soliciting the Partners on a twenty- or thirty-dollar daily basis.

He didn't stop soliciting the small donations, though. He kept on doing it, right on along with the asking for big pledges.

He had it all worked out as to what percentage he needed on a certain idea or project before he could get started. He'd say, "The percentage I get here is the percentage I won't have to get later."

Jim was very confident after the telethon. Almost overconfident.

I had heard that to operate successfully, the hotel should have 50 percent of the rooms occupied with paying guests.

With all the Partnerships Jim was selling, there was no way he could have half of the rooms *available* for rent to other people. But Jim was sold on the idea that the partners *wouldn't come,* especially the user from California, Hawaii, or other faraway places.

Jim would go on about the Partnerships running out, about sending in your money *now:* "We've only got a thousand Partnerships left . . ." went on for weeks.

It was wild.

After the shows, he'd sell Partnerships to the audience, even though up to 50 percent of the audience already had one. I saw lines of fifteen or twenty people, waiting to give him their $1000. Some people bought many more than one partnership; I heard of one person who bought twelve.

It was superb salesmanship.

People were excited and happy at getting Partnerships, more than thrilled at giving their $1000 for the four-day, three-night package. Guaranteed. It seemed a very small investment to insure a nice yearly vacation for the rest of your life, and you were building something nice for Christians, too. People flocked to do it.

It was like hanging out a piece of meat in front of a dog. Once the dog gets the smell, the dog just has to have it. Jim was selling the sizzle off it, you might say.

It was a phenomenal success, and everybody was happy. People were buying memberships for their children, and for their brothers and sisters.

I'm convinced the money was going into day-to-day expenses, rather than the hotel, because Roe Messner was falling behind in getting paid. All that money coming in, and Roe wasn't getting paid.

It had to be going somewhere.

Still, when Roe would put pressure on them, I'd receive a check from David and take it to him. One of the checks was for over a million dollars. I did this three or four Fridays.

The alterations to the hotel plans kept right on coming. One of the things Jim kept changing was his personal suite. It started at 1000 square feet, but he paid it almost daily visits to revise it, and it ended up being 3,000 square feet.

I never got to see the suite in completion, but it was going to have a large, large living room with stained-glass windows, and lavish furniture. Some French doors, some arched doorways. He was just going to use it to relax in after the shows, or maybe come for a weekend, and he was going to use it for entertaining. It had a real nice dining room. I think they were planning white carpet.

James Taggart, David's brother, was decorating it for them. David told me they were going to pay James $200,000, and were going to put him on a retainer fee after that just for his advice.

Later, when the Towers plans got going, Jim planned the top floor as his penthouse, to use instead of the suite at the Grand.

The Towers idea came into existence during the Heritage Grand telethon. Jim said to David, "We've got to get another project going." And he described the Towers, 500 more rooms. (The Towers were planned as twenty-five stories; I've read in 1987 that they're only twenty-one.) Jim was well aware that it was wrong to ask for money for one thing and spend it on another. He said so more than once in my presence. But if he invented the Towers, and asked for money for "both" the Towers and the Grand, he could throw the Towers money at the Grand.

David said that evening, "To use this money for anything other than the Towers, the money will have to go into the general fund, not the Towers fund." Jim didn't want to hear about money problems. He turned David's concern aside fast.

Jim was well aware that the Feds were looking at his tactics, but felt that PTL's being a religious organization protected them, and he used the television camera to denounce the government. He played religious freedom to the limit. His boldness frightened me as well as made me mad. I understood full well that he was exploiting his position.

Why Jim felt the need for more money is still mysterious in 1987. The Grand's original cost estimate was $25 million. Granted, it soon went up to $30 million; and by the time I left, Jim's changes had pushed it on towards the $40 million mark. But on the Towers alone, PTL raised $70 million, and cost on the Towers to date is pegged at $26 million.

So why is Roe owed $14 million on the Towers and other buildings? Your guess is as good as mine. I will say that Jim was spending money that year the way you and I drink water. It was free and ever-flowing.

Jim told the Partners in September 1984 that "there's no mortgage to pay" on the Partner Center (Heritage Grand). But he took out a $10 million mortgage on it in November of 1984.

So, even forgetting all the money he took in for the Grand, the $70 million for the Towers alone should have covered the $40 million (or so) on the Grand, *plus* the $14 million owed to Roe, *plus* the $12 million Roe got on the Towers, with $4 million left over.

Why a $10 million mortgage? Again, your guess is as good as mine.

David worried at Jim a lot about the money flow at PTL. He said more than once, "You know we couldn't withstand an investigation. We've got to do everything we can to prevent one happening. We beat the FCC," (an investigation had been settled in PTL's favor some time before I got there) "but you know the IRS is just waiting for us."

"Yeah, yeah," Jim would say.

And David would also say, "The Finance Department's awfully concerned about what money's going where," hoping to get Jim to do something about it.

Sometimes Jim blew up: "They work for me! They ought to do what I tell them. Why do they question me?"

They were right to question him. I myself understood that at least part of the money solicited for the Towers was going to go to the Grand. I knew then— even before I saw how sincerely Jim could squander money on personal things—the ministry would fall one day. You can't run a "Ponzi scheme," as PTL attorney Roy Grutman called it in 1987—paying off the first project with money raised for the second project—forever. I often said that if Jim ever ran out of ideas, he would certainly be exposed. He had to keep things confusing, even as far as some of the staff were concerned.

After I left, Jim went on selling Partnerships in the Towers, and he added other projects, too—bunkhouses, farmhouses, a thirty-room "country club" mansion and "country club" camping. None of those ever got done—although the grand total that came in for offers of free lodging and other benefits, including the Heritage Grand and the Towers, was $160 million.

It's just a mind-bending amount of money.

And the present management of PTL says there's no way they can honor the promises of free lodging; depending on how you count it, Jim oversold the available space by at least 500 percent. That is, Heritage U.S.A. would have to have five *times* as many rooms and campsites as it does, just to accommodate the people who sent in their money!

Actually, the present PTL management says the people who sent in their money didn't buy anything. They sent gifts, the present management says, and they have no legal claim against PTL. But PTL's present Chief Operating Officer, Harry Hargrave, added during a bankruptcy hearing, "Morally we don't think it is right" to leave the Partners with nothing.

The ad that PTL ran in the May/June 1984 issue of *Together, the Magazine for PTL Club Partners*, does say "gift," but it emphasizes what you'll get.

Under the headline "Stay Here FREE . . . Every Year . . . All Your Life!" the ad says, "You and your family can stay in the beautiful world-class Heritage Grand Hotel FREE for four days and three nights EACH YEAR for the rest of your life, when you become a PTL Lifetime Partner, giving a one-time gift of $1000. . . . This special program is already nearly filled, so it's very important that you act right away to ensure free lodging for you and your family every year for the rest of your life. . . . Lifetime Partners may also use annual FREE lodging by staying five days and four nights at the luxurious Heritage Inn, or camping eleven days and ten nights in one of five camp loops."

Seems to me that if I'd answered that ad by sending in my money, I'd surely have *thought* I was buying something. . . .

There was more building that year.

The big outdoor amphitheater already existed, of course, with its 3500 seats. But that spring a total redesign was going on, to make it right for the first

Dear Friend,

Each day, I am filled with more and more excitement
as I see our PTL Partner Center nearing completion.
God gave me a vision for a worldwide Christian
center years ago, and finally, we are seeing it
fulfilled!

Until now, Heritage USA has not been the fellowship
center I have always dreamed of. Facilities have
been too spread out, there has not been enough
lodging, and Partners like you have not had a common
place to gather together to shop, eat, relax,
fellowship and worship.

Last year alone, we had to turn away 150,000 people
because we did not have enough room in the Heritage
Inn -- that's enough people to fill the Heritage
Grand Hotel for a year!

When the PTL Partner Center is completed this
summer, it will be the only center of its kind
anywhere in the world ... and it is built exclusively for you and your family to enjoy!

The Bible says, " ... but the people that do know
their God shall be strong, and do exploits" (Daniel
11:32). I believe that this PTL Partner Center is
truly a great exploit in the name of our God!
Millions of people have needed a godly place to come
to for years, and now we have the Christian alterna-
tive for them!

I hope you will be able to join us for the dedication of the PTL Partner Center on July 4. I know

this celebration will signal one of the greatest moments in the PTL ministry, and I want you to be a part of it.

But you don't have to wait until this summer to be a part of the PTL Partner Center. You can join us today as a PTL Lifetime Partner with a gift of $1,000, and stay in the Heritage Grand Hotel for 4 days and 3 nights ... for the rest of your life!

I know you will be proud to be one of the Lifetime Partners who helped build the most magnificent fellowship center of its kind, and you will be able to enjoy the wonderful benefits of Lifetime Partnership for the rest of your life.

Our Lifetime Partnerships are going fast, so we need to hear from you today! We look forward to you joining the celebration with us this summer at the brand new PTL Partner Center!

In warmest Christian love,

Jim Bakker

Passion Play that summer. Very elaborate permanent work was done on the stage area, rocks to look like Calvary, a garden area for Gethsemane. It wasn't cheap.

It was very effective. The first night of the Passion Play, we'd set aside an enclosed area for Jim, where he could watch the play in private. He'd have none of it; he wanted to be down with the people. So I took him and Tammy down among the audience, in the lively, exciting event, the music, the lights, the actors. It seemed like the heart of life beating that night. Even the fact that it rained on us didn't dampen the occasion.

In 1984, the PTL Home, the home for unwed mothers, got started. Jim was asking for money for that, too. Later in the spring he was really beating the bushes for the Home. In the May/June issue of *Together, the Magazine for PTL Club Partners*, Jim said:

"With the People That Love Home 90 percent, complete, construction was suddenly halted because of lack of funds. In the midst of this crisis, the Holy Spirit told me, *'Jim, the reason PTL has hit this impasse is because the Devil is the Prince of Death.'* This home means life for many of America's unborn babies.

"In a great Victory Service we took authority in the name of Jesus, claiming completion of the PTL home totally debt free. Now we must have the help of many faithful PTL Partners . . . immediately . . . to take the final step of victory!"

It was in May and June that I watched the Bakkers spend well over $200,000 on personal indulgences, as I describe for you later. Think that money might have helped the last 10 percent of construction? I do.

In mid-June of 1987 the Bakkers said they were down to their last $37,000. A month later they were reported as spending $300,000 to remodel their Gatlinburg, Tennessee, house. I guess it's the same old thing.

Well. The Victory Service on the PTL Home was really something. We were making the show out there that day. Jim liked to run shows from various construction sites, and the staff hated it. It meant working all night usually the night before, prettying up the grounds, getting all the lights and cameras ready.

After the show, when Jim was hanging around talking to the audience, he seemed to get the idea for the Victory March all at once. He was going to expel the Devil from the building. There were over a thousand people there. He persuaded them to line up like a train, everybody holding the shoulder or waist of the person ahead. The band struck up rousing march music, and I fell into line three or four people behind Jim, who was leading, of course. We wound all in through the building, and all around it, for about half an hour, chanting "Hallelujah!" and "Praise the Lord!"; and we prayed for victory over this building. Afterwards Jim proclaimed victory.

I felt like a fool in that line, sashaying along, but I couldn't help grinning.

In the summer I gave an idea to producer Bobbie Garn for a very successful ad for the home: to use the song "Kids" by the Oak Ridge Boys on the sound track. I understand the spot won some kind of award.

Bobbie won awards for her next two spots, too. She was on a roll. It seemed to me then, and still does, that Bobbie has more unused talent than most Hollywood producers have all together.

The home did get built, and the first few girls moved in before I left. It was a stone and wood structure, with an inner courtyard and a large stone fireplace.

Jim seemed very sincere about the need for the Home for Unwed Mothers. He thought these girls would benefit from being in a good Christian environment. He set up the Tender Loving Care Adoption Agency there to find good homes for the babies. I was not aware of any child-care classes, or any academic classes, for the girls, although apparently they were later offered further education and part-time employment. They were expected to do volunteer work around the grounds. It had room for about three dozen girls.

Jim said the home and the adoption agency would both be licensed by the state of South Carolina, and according to *Heritage Village Church*, the home did get licensed, and the agency became fully accredited.

CHAPTER 6

The elders which are among you. . . . Feed the flock of God, which is among you . . . being ensamples to the flock.

I PETER 5:1

The year of 1984 saw a huge inpouring of money, and a huge building program.

Who was in charge?

Jim Bakker.

Jim had a board, but here's how the board operated.

Board meetings were held once a quarter. I was in and out of them, bringing this, going to get that.

At the time Efrem Zimbalist, Jr., the noted movie and television actor; Aimee Cortese, pastor of an Assemblies of God church and sometime prison chaplain; and A. T. Lawing, a Charlotte businessman and founder of the Charlotte Oil and Equipment Company, were on the board. There was also Charles H. Cookman, District Superintendent for the North Carolina Assemblies of God—the district in which Jim had been ordained in 1964, and the district which, in 1987, had to deal with dismissing Jim from the ministry.

Richard Dortch was on the board for five years before he joined the PTL in December 1983; he attended board meetings after that, but whether he was still a board member, I don't know.

Richard Dortch came to PTL as number-two man under Jim. The press said in 1987, he came in the wake of allegations of misuse of PTL money.

His last prior job was as Illinois District Superintendent for the Assemblies of God, a position he had held for thirteen years. He had also been, for fourteen years, one of the Executive Presbyters of the denomination. I heard that he'd expected to be elected General Superintendent in 1983, and his failure to do so was a main reason for his joining PTL.

Richard Dortch was going to live in a house that belonged to PTL out on Lake Wylie, a considerable distance from the Bakker house. PTL went in and spent somewhere in the neighborhood of $500,000 remodeling this house for Dortch, buying all brand-new furniture, tearing out rooms, adding on things, redoing the yard and the pool. They provided him a Cadillac Seville, navy blue.

As soon as he arrived (with his wife, his divorced daughter Deanna, and Deanna's young son, who lived with them), he began getting PTL people to go out and clean his pool, clean his house, clean his boat—things like that.

It seemed to me that the minute he saw Jim had something, he had to have one too. Like that boat.

Jim had a houseboat, a big one.

Next thing you know, Dortch has a houseboat, too.

The board meetings began with an elaborate lunch—once, I remember, the meat course was a steamboat roast of beef that must have weighed twenty pounds. The food was catered up from the Wagon Wheel Restaurant to the president's office, served in the boardroom on the big glass-topped table. The chairs were white-upholstered high-backs; really nice.

After an hour or so of food, and chat, Jim would get down to business. He'd present drawings of the next things he planned to build—selling his dreams to them. I never saw the board act as if they had any power, or as if they disapproved of Jim's plans in any way. They just seemed to be there to be told what was going to be done. What Jim wanted to do.

Efrem Zimbalist, Jr. seldom attended. When he did, he seemed preoccupied.

A. T. Lawing, a silver-haired, tall, formally dressed man who was fond of cowboy boots, was very laid back. His characteristic attitude was: "Fine, Jim, whatever you want to do."

Richard Dortch kept quiet. When he tried to put his two cents in, here or elsewhere, saying, "We're going to . . ." you could see Jim didn't like it. Jim just wanted to tell what *his* ideas were.

Aimee Cortese, who was five-foot-six and a very heavy woman, was full of life and nice things to say. She herself was pastor of a church in the Bronx. She spoke up often in board meetings, with suggestions that seemed to make a lot of sense to me—but I never saw Jim follow any of them. She didn't criticize Jim; her suggestions were on details of his plans. I liked dark-haired Aimee. She had a daughter who was one of the Heritage Singers.

I didn't know that Aimee had at least one very special meeting on PTL's behalf while I was there—a meeting with Jessica Hahn in March. She'd meet with her again in November 1984, and *The Charlotte Observer* reported in 1987 that Aimee persuaded Hahn to sign a statement recanting her accusations against Jim.

Aimee received a copy of the papers with which Hahn threatened lawsuit, but turned them over to Dortch. She didn't say anything to the Assemblies of God about the Hahn incident; as an Assemblies of God pastor herself, Aimee was liable to church reprimand for this, but in June 1987 the Assemblies had not decided whether to take action against her.

At one point in 1987, a New York newspaper suggested that Aimee might have bankrolled the PTL payment to Hahn, but Aimee emphatically denied it altogether.

The press also reports, however, that PTL gave Aimee's church a $50,000 donation not long after the payoff to Hahn was arranged.

And the press has reported that all the payoff money was funneled through Roe Messner's firm, Commercial Builders, at Dortch's request. Roe's firm paid out the $265,000, and then submitted invoices for that amount.

While I was in the boardroom I never heard discussion of Jim's and Tammy's salaries. After one meeting, though, Jim came out and said the board had given them raises.

Board, hell, I thought. You just gave yourself a raise

and told the board that. From the way they rubber-stamped his every move, I just couldn't believe they were controlling his take. I was aware of *so* many bonuses!

The meetings lasted a couple of hours. Sometimes they'd be followed by a tour of new construction. We'd fetch a limo and carry them around.

PTL had three limos, Cadillacs, and they bore Texas and Ohio tags. Jim's and Tammy's cars had Ohio tags, too. While I was there they sent off for new tags—again out of state.

Richard Dortch was a hard-nosed businessman with a stern and autocratic manner. From the first day, he showed that he wanted to control the PTL purse strings. David Taggart got very upset, more nervous than usual.

Dortch brought in a new man to be Director of the Financial Department, and a new Director of Personnel. (Vi Azvedo didn't seem to mind; she had a great deal of other stuff going on, the workshops and seminars, as well as her important job of making sure that Jim and Tammy were happy, encouraging them to reward themselves for their great achievements, smoothing over marital spats.)

Dortch also hired his own son—or perhaps I should say, put his son on the PTL payroll—and brought in Eric Watt, the young (mid-twenties) son of former Secretary of the Interior James Watt, to be head of the fifteen to twenty PTL pastors, as well as installing his own Director of Music, Paul Ferrin.

David Taggart loathed this. "We're in the age of the Dortchites!" he would shriek.

David was an interesting guy. In his late twenties,

he made $360,000 in 1986. He worked very hard. He'd get into the office at 8:00 A.M. or before, and he usually didn't leave until 7:00 or 8:00 at night.

He'd worked for PTL before 1984, then left and gone to Florida. He'd come back only a little while before I arrived.

David was tall and slim, with sharp features and a flamboyant personality.

Often people wondered where David got the money to live in the lavish manner he did; he told me and his other acquaintances that his father had a Cadillac dealership in Detroit.

David and his brother James, who was near him in age, and who also worked for PTL, had the most gorgeous clothes I ever saw on men. They could (and did) wear the same clothes, although James was a little heavier than David, particularly around the rump. Imagine *GQ* magazine—they had everything in it. Once David wanted to show me the closet in their two-bedroom Charlotte condo that James had just redecorated. They had a lot of black and crystal ornaments, a baby grand piano, and a lot of mirrors.

The downstairs bedroom just had odds and ends in it—no bed. They seemed to use it for storage.

Upstairs, I noticed that the bedroom had only one bed, a king-size.

The closet James had planned was really something. It was a large walk-in, arranged so that the shoes, suit, shirts, sweaters, and ties that went together (for their shoes matched or coordinated with their suits) were placed together, all ready to select.

It looked more like a clothing store than a closet.

Their shoes were Gucci, or very expensive-looking

French or other Italian styles. I remember particularly one cream-colored suit, double-breasted like many of their suits, that was out of this world. The shirts were all colors.

David's jewelry was something. He had a big gold ring with a big diamond that he told me cost $86,000. His Cartier watch—James had one too—was a very dainty thing, with a sharkskin band; David told me it cost $20,000.

David carried two small Louis Vuitton cases—pocketbook size—daily. One case held three bottles of Valium, as well as other containers of what looked like pills and tablets. The other Vuitton case held his jewels—bracelets, rings, gold chains. He told me once that the jewelry was worth "over half a million."

All sorts of thoughts ran through my head. First I thought he must be lying. Then I thought, if he was telling the truth, he was surely stupid. What if somebody found out about it and tried to rob him? I guess he didn't want to leave it at home, but he also liked to change his jewelry during the day.

James was an interior decorator, and his work was good. David told me he was paid $200,000 for decorating Jim and Tammy's suite at the Heritage Grand. James was said to be a pretty good cook, but they seemed to eat out every night, usually around eleven or midnight because David worked very late at PTL. Their favorite restaurant was Café Eugene, one of the most elegant places in the Charlotte area.

Two or three times a week David would take PTL people who worked with the executives out for a good dinner. They invited me often. Sometimes I went. I don't remember whether we went in James's Mercedes or David's—it was the cream-colored one.

James was good company, very funny.

I remember one night when David said, "You *must* try the filet mignon." I did, and boy, it really melted in the mouth. After dinner I was sitting there drinking wine that had cost $100 a bottle, and it was *wonderful.* David had been a concert pianist, and that night we—James and Penny Hollenbeck and I—persuaded him to play the piano. He played beautifully for forty-five minutes, never looking at a book or a note.

I had a great time that evening, except for a few minutes of terror when I suddenly thought, "They *are* paying for this meal, aren't they?" There was no way I could have paid for it. I couldn't have afforded it, either. But they did pay, of course, and left a generous tip, too.

David was used to drawing the expense money for Jim's trips, and told me more than once the funds were never accounted. "If they want to keep their jobs down there (in the Finance Department), they *better* not ask."

On trips he also did the signing for credit cards. Jim and Tammy didn't worry themselves with keeping tabs on the money; they just spent it.

After Dortch had been there awhile, David told me that Dortch was planning to oust another executive, and me, too, because we were too close to Jim, and replace us with his own candidates. I paid no attention. I was sure that Jim respected the other candidate for ousting, who was a friend of mine, and would never fire him. And I myself had done nothing to be fired for.

When my friend heard about this rumor, though, he was very upset. He was super-loyal to Jim, but he apparently didn't trust Jim not to fire him. This surprised me, and saddened me.

The friend said that all people who got close to Jim were fired sooner or later. He told me of one man who'd been fired, and who said he wouldn't leave the grounds until he'd talked to Jim.

My friend was called and told to get him off the property. My friend had done it, but he hadn't forgotten it.

After a while my friend's worry about Dortch blew over. But not before he had agonized a whole lot.

Jim had trouble believing David sometimes. Once in the car, he and Tammy were talking about something David had said, and Jim commented, "It's hard to know how much faith to put in it. David might just be in another one of his bitchy moods."

Once David saw that Dortch was going to be satisfied with control of funds up to the president's office, but not including it, he relaxed some. But if anything at all went wrong, David's first cry was, "Dortch has screwed up again!"

David himself never admitted to having made a mistake—at least in my hearing.

Sometimes Dortch hosted the television shows. He always wanted very heavy makeup for them. I thought of it as his war paint. I guess he hoped it made him look younger.

He was about fifty-two, a heavyset man, with glasses and silvery hair . . . what there was of it. He had bad stomach problems, and he was supposed to watch his diet very carefully. He didn't, although he did drink a lot of milk. He was a passionate St. Louis Cardinals fan. The baseball Cardinals.

Dortch was a smiler, forever giving me a pat on the back, asking how I was. I didn't trust him.

In 1987, Dortch said he had a memorandum he'd sent Jim when he was joining PTL, saying it promised him $25,000 more each year than the salary and benefits he'd had as Illinois District Superintendent of the Assemblies of God. *The Charlotte Observer* said that would have made his take at PTL about $135,000 a year.

The reason this was in the paper after Jim left PTL, after Dortch was dismissed as President of PTL, and after Dortch was defrocked by the Assemblies of God on May 6, 1987, was that Dortch was saying PTL should give him some more, because Jim had made a five-year deal with him and he was second-ranking officer of PTL for only three and a half years.

Dortch had $350,000 in 1986, and $270,000 in the first three months of 1987, for a total of $620,000, according to the press. I don't know how much he made in 1984 and 1985, but it seems to me Dortch has had a lot already.

CHAPTER 7

Make a Joyful Noise unto the Lord
PSALM 100:1

Sometimes Heritage U.S.A. seemed a never-ending celebration. Jim wanted it to feel that way, I'm sure. It really was a world within a world.

He spent a lot of money—and a lot of staff effort—on special events to draw people. And it worked. There'd been over 500,000 visitors in 1982, and nearly two million in 1983. (The count was up to 6.1 million visitors in 1986.) Heritage U.S.A. was, by 1986, the third most popular theme park in the country, right after Disneyland and Disney World.

Although *Time* said in August 1987 that Bakker "tailor(ed) his message to the newfound affluence of the Sunbelt," Jim drew his support from *all* parts of the country.

Is Minnesota meant to be part of the Sunbelt? Or Michigan? Not that I've ever heard. And remember when there used to be a Bible Belt?

There are all these fancy labels that people think up.

Jim and Tammy are from Michigan and Minnesota, after all.

And there is no way Heritage U.S.A. was just southern. Just as at Disney World and Disneyland, people came from thousands of miles away. They came to see the shows live, to stay for a while, and to take part in the special events.

The first special event I encountered was also the most elaborate: Christmas City. There were different events planned every night of December, music shows, Christmas plays, something going on in the Barn all the time.

But that was just the beginning.

During Christmas City—which lasted from the beginning of December to about the end of January—all of Heritage U.S.A. was hung with Christmas lights.

We had a single two-lane road, one way in and one way out. It was about a six-mile drive to go all the way in to the back of the property where the Barn and studio were located, and to come back out.

All along the road, if you can imagine this, there were Christmas lights, just millions of them, all over the trees and buildings.

They had a thing called Candy Cane Lane with twenty-foot wooden candy canes, big gingerbread men, and arches of lights across the road.

Next to a big tower made to look like a Christmas tree, a big crane (which had been there for years) was freshly painted yellow, and a real fire engine was brought in and parked. Giant boxes in bright colors made it look like a kid's dream of Christmas morning.

On Angel Boulevard the trees were lit in blue and white.

An angel was installed on top of the water tower. Her body was a metal frame. Lights were looped around the frame—white, of course—and when darkness fell you could see her for a long way. Paul King was in charge of the angel project; Jimmy Swain oversaw all of Christmas City.

The Outreach Center itself, pyramidal in shape, was trimmed up like a Christmas tree.

Santa's Workshop and other displays, some making toys, some cutting wood, some like penguins at the North Pole, involved thirty or forty animated animals. I heard that their cost was $3000 to $4000 each.

It must have cost many hundreds of thousands of dollars for all those lights and electric lines, even though many people donated their time to do the lights. I heard that the electric bill was $100,000 for December. I could believe it.

The lights would be turned on at dusk, and they stayed on until at least midnight. Sometimes they were on *all* night. And didn't the people come to see! Even people who hated the idea of Bakker, and didn't want PTL anywhere around, couldn't resist.

It was beautiful. It was like being in a Christmas card. There were people on hayrides, there were people out there caroling, shopping; the air was full of music. It was so happy to see.

The crowds were really big.

So were the traffic problems. We put *all* the guards on evening duty, we marked the way in and way out, but nothing helped. One car would overheat, and until we could push it off the road, everybody else would be backed up behind it.

Most nights traffic was backed up from the front gate of PTL all the way up to the Interstate a mile away, and even *on* the Interstate some nights! I had to meet with the Highway Patrol because of the problems the traffic was causing—and after a while they started putting patrolmen out there to help us get the people in and out.

It was chaos.

Jim thrived on it. The more people he could get down there, no matter how much money it cost, the happier he was. Seeing the people made him feel he was doing the right thing.

But also, he just loved Christmas City. A lot of nights he wouldn't go home until nine or ten; a lot of nights when he had gone home, he'd want to come back from the house just to look.

He'd say, "Stop. Look at that gingerbread man. Isn't that something!" And he'd twist around in his seat like a kid, enjoying it all, and he'd say, "I wish I could have seen stuff like this when I was a kid."

Sometimes he'd bring Jamie Charles down there to enjoy it, but Jamie Charles never seemed quite so excited as Jim was.

Of course, Jamie Charles had grown up in wealth. Jim had not. He wrote in *Move that Mountain* that his dad "made a decent living." Mr. Raleigh Bakker was a machinist in a piston-ring plant. "But I thought we lived in poverty. . . . It seemed like anything I had was inferior to what other kids had. Year after year I wore the same tattered blue baseball jacket with prominent white stitching, until the stitching unraveled completely. . . . I became filled with deep-seated feelings of inferiority."

He couldn't get enough of Christmas City.

And it was free, you know. A lot of the people who came there were really poor. I'm sure, for some of them, it was the only Christmas they had.

"Makes you feel like a little kid again, doesn't it?" he'd say to me, squirming around like one himself.

And it did. I loved him for making Christmas City. I just wish it could all have been like that.

It was a huge amount of work getting Christmas City ready, even with all the volunteer help, and some things fell behind.

One was the special toy store Jim wanted set up at the amphitheater. It wasn't ready. We went down there one day, and he threw himself around for two hours, whipping everything into shape, and suddenly it was done. Everything completely set up and decorated.

He just marveled at what he had done. We got back in the car, and he just laughed at the way that people had jumped around when he yelled orders. After it was over, he bragged that if he wanted anything done he would just have to do it himself.

I was amazed then, as I often was, at how brilliant he was at pulling their finest work out of people. People would go to any lengths to please him. But that toy store afternoon upset me, too: I couldn't help thinking of Christ throwing the money changers out of the temple, and there Jim was, seeing that the cash registers were set up.

But what hurts me most is thinking about the hard-working—no, overworked—staff just then. Employees would complain to me about the long hours—but the complainers were never, it seemed to me, the people who had the worst of it. It made me really angry then, and I'd say, "I don't give a damn. He's the reason you're here. If you don't like what's demanded of you, then quit!"

Those words haunt me now.

Christmas was the time of year that Jim loved best. He didn't seem to want a lot of presents for himself; he genuinely wanted everyone around him to be happy—that was his present. He, and Tammy, too, never wanted Christmas to end.

I guess it went with his "prosperity theology" ideas that, if you pray and give, you'll get rich; but I think he really wanted everybody to have Christmas all year long. He was nice to be around at Christmastime.

Easter wasn't anything special at Heritage U.S.A. I think there was a simple Easter-egg hunt for the kids, and the service that Sunday was banked with lilies, but Easter wasn't a time that PTL made a whole lot of fuss over.

The next big carrying-on was the Fourth of July.

Heritage U.S.A. didn't just have a fancy weekend; it was a *nine-day* celebration.

"All-day worship services with parades and fireworks are part of our 'Passover,' a time each year when we remember how God has miraculously delivered us from our enemies," *Heritage Village Church* says. "A day of rejoicing throughout Heritage U.S.A. as we celebrate our heritage and the great victories won."

In July 1984, there was supposed to be the opening

Jim and Tammy in their North Central Bible College
sweatshirts a couple of months before their marriage in
1961.

Jim and Tammy in 1962 pose with a congregation in Falling Waters, West Virginia.

Jim and Tammy in the early 1960s—before the makeup and the money.

Jim's parents, Raleigh and Furnia, at their home at Heritage USA.

The human Christmas tree. Jim loved Christmas and went out of his way to make it extra special.

The twenty-fifth anniversary party for Jim and Tammy. This was a gala event sponsored by PTL members to "honor the Bakkers for their leadership and faithfulness."

Tammy Faye hosting her show *Tammy's House Party*.

Jim shown here with President Reagan.

Jim and Tammy stand proudly in front of Heritage USA.

A shot of the spectacular water park at Heritage USA,
which was not finished until after I left the PTL.

The Heritage USA train. Sitting directly behind Tammy is
Richard Dortch.

Aimee Garcia Cortese, the PTL board member from the Bronx.

Vi Azvedo, shown here counseling married couples. Tammy and Jim credited her with saving their marriage.

Reverend Dortch shown here with his family at home. With his gray hair and easy warmth, he exuded a comforting fatherly image.

Several posed family pictures of Jim and Tammy with their children, Tammy Sue and Jamie Charles.

Tammy Sue, who aspired to follow in her mother's musical footsteps. She eloped this year.

"Lust took me by surprise."

The Rolls Royce Bakker purchased in 1984.

Mike in his official PTL
security guard uniform.

Mike Richardson.

of the Heritage Grand, but that didn't get done on time. There was, however, a giant Fourth of July Victory Parade, a huge fireworks show, a mammoth picnic, special Bible seminars, special concerts, and the Passion Play.

I don't remember much about the parade, because Jim was leading it and I was right behind him. It was big, though, complete with floats.

The city of Charlotte was having fireworks for the Fourth, too, and Jim was determined that the PTL show should be better.

The fireworks were stupendous. I heard the figure $50,000 attached to them. I have never seen a greater display.

Jim was the M.C. of the show, from a specially built platform on the lake. I took him and Tammy and their guests over there by boat. Phil Driscoll, a well-known trumpet player, provided the stirring music for the show.

There was a loud misfire that night while the technicians were setting off the fireworks, and it could have been a real tragedy. It was pure luck that no one was hurt or killed. Jim was very concerned about it, and kept asking me what had happened, worrying about the people being all right. I lied to him, and told him it had been nothing. I didn't want him to keep being scared. After all, nothing *had* happened.

They said they had 40,000 people there that night, and I certainly believe it.

The picnic had food you could buy, but you could also bring your own. I estimate that several thousand people were there.

There was a big auction at the Auction Barn as part

of the celebration. They had auctions there quite often. They'd started them because Tammy Faye liked flea markets, and Jim thought other people would, too. Bob Johnson was in charge of finding the things to be auctioned, and they used donations, too. It was just every kind of thing you could imagine, by no means all expensive.

Anyway, they had a big special one during the Fourth celebration.

The Fourth was followed immediately by the James Robison Crusade.

Jim didn't want trouble with other evangelists. To the contrary, he had a sincere desire for all evangelists to get along, whatever their individual differences might be. As Jim saw it, each evangelist might have his own philosophy, but the ultimate goal was the same.

For example, if two families were going to Miami, one might choose to go by Florida's East Coast highway, and the other might choose the West Coast route, turning east on the Tamiami Trail, but the final destination would be the same.

The ultimate goal for all evangelists, of course, would be to bring souls to Christ.

That seemed to be Jim's position on the matter. I never heard him say anything bad about other ministries—although he did express distrust of one or two of them.

Jim seemed to think about Jimmy Swaggart a good deal in 1984. The two men had different ideas of evangelism. Jimmy Swaggart had a school of evangelism—and Swaggart's primary fund-raising effort that year was for his educational effort. He placed his main emphasis, it seemed to me, on training ministers and teaching.

Jim's interest was more along the lines of recreation for Christians, interwoven with teaching.

From what I understood, Jimmy Swaggart would not meet Jim on middle ground. Swaggart evidently would not accept Jim's ideas of ministry as being different from, but just as good as, Swaggart's.

After Jim went to Washington in the spring of 1984 to meet George Bush, where twenty or so evangelists had been in the same room together, I heard him saying that he had hoped that this would be a first step in bringing all the evangelists together, especially him and Swaggart. He had hoped to begin to build a mutual respect with Swaggart, a respect for each other and each other's ministry.

I personally liked the singing that Jimmy Swaggart presented in his shows on television in 1983 and 1984.

Although I listened to Jimmy Swaggart, and other evangelists, and Jim himself, I never gave to any of them. I did give to the Salvation Army, the United Way, and Muscular Dystrophy. I had read enough about the finances of those groups to feel confident that my donations would really go to help people.

I myself couldn't understand, while I was at PTL, why there had to be so many splits among the evangelists, since they *were* all working for the same goal; and it seemed to me that, just as Jim said, criticism of one evangelist by another just bred more discontent in the religious community in general.

Now, looking back, it seems to me that Jimmy

Swaggart and the other evangelists who would not accept Jim were wiser than I was.

In September 1986, Jimmy Swaggart found himself in possession of some unpleasant knowledge.

It was then that John Wesley Fletcher, the man who had introduced Jim to Jessica Hahn, told Swaggart of the Bakker-Hahn meeting for the first time. Swaggart, according to *Time* magazine, asked to meet with Jim.

Instead, Richard Dortch came to see Swaggart and two officials of the Assemblies of God: "I confronted Dortch about the Jessica Hahn thing," Swaggart said, according to *Time*. "He flatly denied it. He lied to me."

In February, at the convention of National Religious Broadcasters, "Swaggart was about to speak when the Rev. John Ankerberg, Southern Baptist proprietor of a weekly TV show, approached, knelt down, and whispered to him that *The Charlotte Observer* was hot on the Bakker-Hahn story," *Time* reported. "Shortly thereafter, Swaggart alerted Assemblies of God leaders to the impending scandal."

Time also reported that in early March Swaggart and Ankerberg, with other evangelists, decided to write to Bakker, asking him "to tell the truth and repent." Swaggart later wrote Ankerberg asking that his name be kept off the letter.

On March 19, Bakker resigned from PTL, and to the surprise of many handed control over to Jerry Falwell.

There was a flurry of accusations that Swaggart had been trying to take over PTL for himself, but Jerry

Falwell seemed to put an end to them quickly, saying that Swaggart had "no designs" on PTL.

Jimmy Swaggart did not come to PTL while I was there, but evangelist James Robison did.

Robison's Crusade followed right after the Fourth of July.

James Robison was a Texas evangelist, from the Dallas–Fort Worth area. He and Jim had had some big falling-out prior to 1984, and Jim saw it as a victory that Robison was coming on his turf—and even better, that Robison apologized for having said some harsh things abut PTL. Jim always felt good when people came to him.

Robison was a good crusader, a very different kind of preacher from Jim. I went to three or four of his meetings in the Barn.

He was a big man, around six-foot-four, with dark hair. He dressed conservatively, in navy blue suits.

He was a more conservative preacher than Jim. He spoke more logically, and struck me as a teacher rather than a salesman. He'd explain so you could follow him.

He made drama out of quietness. He'd pull up a chair to the edge of the audience, and say, very softly, "Listen. Listen to what I'm saying." Or he'd kneel down on one knee, and almost whisper to the people.

Oh, he'd get fired up sometimes, but he created a real intimacy with the people.

I liked the way he was friendly to everyone he met. He didn't ignore people when he was offstage, either. He brought his wife and daughter with him, and his daughter—who was in her late teens—sang one night, I remember. His wife was conservatively dressed. I liked the way they seemed with each other.

All during this time it was mass confusion. Hot weather. And wall-to-wall people.

Even when nothing special was going on, every day at Heritage U.S.A. was special to the people who came there. Quiet, but Christian, as they saw it, and special.

If you wanted to, you could start your day with a walk through a pretty country setting in the woods or on the lakeside. Then maybe visit the Upper Room for morning prayer.

A nice breakfast at the Wagon Wheel, country style, on the lake, followed by an early Bible seminar or service, and it's ten o'clock, time to head over to the studio and get a good seat for *The Jim Bakker Show*. Then you could head out for lunch at McMoose's, the fast-food restaurant, or the Little Horse for a sandwich or full meal, or pick up some pizza at the Youth Center. Then on to an afternoon seminar—on marriage, or the single life, or inner healing.

After that maybe a swim in one of the two huge swimming pools, or maybe Tammy's show (if you were there before it was canceled), and then some supper. The day would wind up with a camp meeting back at the Barn.

A lot of people liked days just like that.

But there was plenty of other stuff to do, too.

There were tennis courts, and miniature golf. At the Youth Center there were video games and a pool table, and Buffalo Park had a playground area and shallow pool for kids.

At Heritage Farms there was a petting zoo, with ducks, chickens, cows, and other animals. Two camels were at the farms, too; we used them for the Passion Play. But I don't think they let anybody pat them. Camels are mean. They bite—and they spit.

You could also rent horses to ride.

On the lake, there were canoes, and paddleboats, and you could fish. I saw people fishing; I don't remember anybody catching anything.

And there were bicycles, too.

In 1984 Jim began work on the Water Park. It was a big plan, and would feature its own mountain, sixty feet tall. He had found a water park that was supposed to be the biggest and best in the world, and planned to make his even bigger. He always wanted everything of his to be the biggest and the best.

To begin with, Jim had to dredge a new canal on the lake edge next to the Heritage Grand. Using the fill from this new inlet, he built up the spit of land between the inlet and the lake itself, and with dirt and Gunite built the mountain. There would be several water slides down from the top, and at the bottom would be lots of coves and inlets so people could pick the depth of water they wanted to be in.

The whole bottom "lake" would have waves, made by hydraulic machinery. It was just going to be a wonderful place to celebrate being alive.

The Water Park wasn't opened that year, but when it was, it was very popular. There are usually about sixty lifeguards on duty there, just as Jim said there would be.

Just as the world of the lake at Heritage U.S.A. was simpler then, so was the shopping. Once the Grand

...ed, there was the whole Main Street U.S.A. str..t of shops, but in 1984 you could browse in a Tammy Faye clothing store, and a men's clothing store, and the General Store had gifts, including Bibles, and inspirational tapes, and Jim and Tammy's books.

Charlotte Whiting, the vice-president Jim called "my personal do-er," was in charge of the shops, but she also handled projects Jim wanted done right and done fast. She was in charge of redoing Dortch's house, for instance.

Charlotte was a slim, petite blonde in her fifties, who dressed well in conservative suits. She had the respect of everyone I knew at PTL. She was spunky; she'd tell Jim he was putting too much work on her, and she could tell him her critical opinions on things without getting fired.

She'd been with the ministry a long time. She didn't need to work; her husband, who has since died, was wealthy. She was loyal to Jim. Although she disapproved of the lavish spending the Bakkers were doing, and disapproved of the money spent on the Dortch residence, she believed in the ministry. For her, it seemed, the good things outweighed the bad. And PTL gave her a place to belong, a place to accomplish good things.

Charlotte did a very good job on the stores. They were always in good shape.

There were lots of things to do at Heritage U.S.A., but smoking wasn't one of them. There was no smoking on the grounds. Not anywhere.

It was worth your job to be caught smoking. Even off the grounds.

As for alcohol? It just wasn't considered a possibility at PTL. That was the public position at PTL, anyway.

Here's what Tammy wrote in *I Gotta Be Me* about a "small glass of wine" given Tammy and Jim by a friend after their wedding: "Jim and I had never tasted wine before. But just for Lena we each took a sip and I almost gagged. I couldn't even stand the smell of it. It stayed in our refrigerator for weeks before I had the heart to throw it out. We got quite a whiff every time we opened the door."

One afternoon when we were out at the house in Palm Desert, California, Jim was wound up tight about something or other.

Vi Azvedo came to me and said, "I want you to run down to the liquor store and buy a bottle of vodka. Get some orange juice, too. I have to mix Jim up a tonic for the body tonight."

I had never seen Jim take a drink of any kind of alcohol, and this was something he preached very hard against. He just didn't condone drinking, or smoking either. He and Tammy were totally against these things.

Vi continued, "Just make sure that nobody sees what you are doing." She gave me the money.

I drove toward the liquor store feeling very guilty. Not for myself, because although I don't drink hard liquor, I do drink beer and wine, and I don't care who knows it. But I felt guilty about this trip, about hiding what I was doing.

I parked around the corner from the liquor store, afraid somebody would recognize me or the car. I snuck into the store, bought the vodka, and rushed

e car. I felt like God—or somebody—was
wa. g me. It was a bad feeling.

I picked up the orange juice and went on back to
the house.

They were in the kitchen when I came in, Jim and
Tammy and Vi. The fifth of vodka was in a paper bag;
I'd been carrying it by the neck.

Jim and Tammy and Vi and David saw me put it
down on the counter. Now you know a bottle of
booze that's been carried that way doesn't look like
anything but a bottle of booze.

Vi got up from the kitchen table and took out a
glass. She mixed the drink, and handed it to Jim. She
mixed one for herself, too.

All the time she was putting on this big game that
she was pouring Jim a simple orange juice, that she
was hiding the stuff from Jim, but there was no way
he didn't see. He was no more than four feet away
from her.

I think their game was all for me.

She gave it to Jim and he drank it. Not that there's
anything wrong with drinking vodka, in my personal
opinion. It was just that he preached so hard against
it; it was a sin, just a pure sin, to drink it, he'd say. And
here he was drinking.

He kept saying, "Ooh, this is good! What'd you put
in it, Vi?" like he didn't know what it was, and giving
us all little smiles.

There was no way he didn't know. It was a put-on
for my benefit, nothing else but. They must have
thought I was some kind of an idiot.

It made me furious. I went out to the pool. I
wanted to say, "You fool, what are you doing?" By

this time I felt everything I saw was a fake. This wasn't the first time since coming to work for PTL that I had seen something that twisted me up inside. "You're doing what you say is wrong." I sat there awhile, trying to come to grips with this. I was working for the man; I owed him my respect. But I couldn't give it to him. Not anymore.

If I hadn't been all those miles from home, I'd have quit that night, I believe.

He drank vodka on at least three other nights out there, in my presence. What he drank when I wasn't there, I don't know, but I can't believe that he only drank in front of me—not after all the trouble they went to make me think Jim didn't know what he was doing.

After that first night, and my not saying anything to them about the drinks, they didn't put on the games again.

He didn't always drink it with orange juice. At least once Vi mixed it with lime.

Vi drank out there, too, even more often than Jim. She kept liquor in her house in Tega Cay.

Tammy was taking serious amounts of Valium that year, "for her nerves," and we all knew it. She had both blue ones and yellow ones. I personally saw her take Valium more than twenty times—and I wasn't with her all day long the way I was with Jim.

At least twice while I was at PTL, Tammy was taken to California by Vi Azvedo—because she was sick, Vi said. But David said that the Valium was getting to her and she needed to "dry out" some.

I don't know even now, for sure, but I figured the Valium was the real reason she went away.

One day in the summer, she narrowly avoided real trouble. She got a Valium prescription filled, then went right back to the same pharmacy with a second prescription and tried to fill it, too.

The pharmacist wouldn't do it.

The doctor came out to the house and met with Jim and Tammy, and the incident was smoothed over.

This woman had so much potential. I couldn't understand why Jim—or Vi or David, for that matter—didn't see that she received the continuing professional attention that she seemed so clearly to need.

"Drying out" trips to California, if that's what they were, were not nearly enough help for Tammy Faye, or so it seemed to me. She seemed to be living a kind of torment. I wanted to see her get well, and she clearly wasn't.

So many days that year, Tammy couldn't stop talking. It was hard to carry on any conversation with her when she was like that. She was loud, and she would interrupt everything, going off on unconnected tangents. She'd finish Jim's sentences for him. He'd let her, and then he'd resume talking.

Often Tammy Faye seemed not to hear what had just been said, and sometimes she didn't make sense. When she was this way, as she frequently was, she was full of grand but unconnected plans for the future. I seldom saw her when she seemed to be relaxed, except possibly when I gave her the ride home by herself. She was usually hyper, it seemed to me.

David Taggart carried Valium with him, and I

often saw him taking one or more at the end of the day, saying, "You don't *know* what I've been through today!"

He offered me Valiums very frequently. One day I took some from him, just to hush him up. I threw them away once I was outside.

Frequently after the show I saw him offer Valiums to Jim. Jim was very hyper after being on, and it would indeed take him some time to come down.

Sometimes—twenty to thirty times that year—I saw Jim take one. I remember him saying once, "Just give me half a one, David. They're *strong.*" He seemed to know what he was talking about.

In Palm Desert, more than once Jim would take Valium during the day, then have a drink in the evening. This worried me, because I knew it was dangerous to mix the two.

But this was *not* the way PTL partners and visitors and workers lived. They were sober people.

There were a lot of good, sincere volunteers, too. In 1986, there were over 1000, contributing an average of 22,000 hours each month to Heritage U.S.A.

And Heritage U.S.A. itself was a lovely little world within a world. It was like a dream of peace and security.

What I couldn't handle was that inside this world within a world was yet another, smaller world of hypocrisy, mistrust, jealousy, and hatred.

CHAPTER 8

When I was a child . . .
I CORINTHIANS 13:11

Who are Jim and Tammy Bakker?

Jim grew up in Muskegon, Michigan, in the Pentecostal household of his parents, Raleigh and Furnia Bakker.

Jim was one of four children—brothers Bob and Norman, and sister Donna. In *Move that Mountain*, Jim says that Donna was "my close friend . . . she tended to mother me." Bob's death is movingly described in *Survival*, another of Jim's books; both Donna and Norman were part of PTL when I was there, as were Jim's parents.

Mom and Dad Bakker lived in Dogwood Hills, and drove a Ford Escort, an inexpensive car. They never visited Jim and Tammy's house while I was there, nor did Jim and Tammy visit their house. Mom and Dad were busy with Bible study groups or other activities at Heritage U.S.A., and seemed to have their own circle of friends. I don't think they ever missed Jim's show; they had their own special seats, and Jim often started off the show from right next to them.

Once or twice a month we would all have Sunday dinner together at the Wagon Wheel. They were both in their seventies. Mom was petite and simply dressed. Her dark brown hair was obviously colored. She wore dark-framed glasses.

Dad stood five-eight or five-nine, with a mustache and a full head of graying dark hair. He was a funny dresser, likely to wear a plaid shirt with a striped tie and a jacket of another plaid, all in bright colors.

It was very difficult for anyone, even Jim, to get a conversation going with Mom and Dad. They were people of few words. They seemed to be stern, tight-laced, devout Christian folks. It was my impression that Dad Bakker ran, and had always run, a tight household, very conservative on money, unlike Jim.

Having lunch with Mom and Dad Bakker was an honor you received if you sent in a $1000 Lifetime Partnership. They were devoted to the ministry and seemed willing to lunch with the Partners if it would help. These lunches would be in a private dining room at the Wagon Wheel; sometimes Jim would join them.

Later the price—the minimum donation—went up to $2000 or $3000 before you got the lunch. It was something special for the high rollers. I guess I shouldn't have thought of these donors that way, but I did.

Relations between the two families were not close. Once, I remember, Dad and Mom drove up to Michigan. Jim didn't hear about it until a couple of days after they'd left. He was worried, then, because his dad was not young—but his parents made the trip safely.

Why was there no visiting back and forth? I don't know any more than you do, but I suspect that Jim didn't want his parents to see the way he and Tammy were living—all the personal wealth. The Bakkers were people of simple tastes.

The senior Bakkers lived very simply, and I'm convinced they bought their house with their own money. They certainly never, to my knowledge, asked for any special attention from PTL staff.

Jim's brother Norman worked for PTL, welcoming Partners, handing out little gifts to them. He was older than Jim, with an artificial leg, and was a garrulous man. He was good with people, but sometimes he seemed to get on Jim's nerves with his talkativeness, although Jim never criticized him where I could hear. He'd want to come into Jim's dressing room before the show.

Some days, Jim would say, "Keep everybody out today, Mike. I don't want to see anybody."

"Well, Norman's here, Jim. He wants to see you."

"I mean *everybody.*"

Norman was not a powerful person at PTL. He and his wife Dorothy and their two kids lived off grounds in 1984, and I never saw his house; but judging by his car and his clothing, he was not making large amounts of money.

Poor Norman was fired this summer of 1987, and he and Dorothy were told to vacate their PTL-owned house. They must have moved on grounds after I left.

Jim's sister Donna worked in the Financial Department, not a very high-up job. She'd been divorced. She and her teenage son lived in a single-wide mobile home just outside the property. Very low-key, she dressed very modestly. She seemed glad to be where she was. She was truly fond of Jim, and he of her. I never saw her either condone Jim's behavior or express disapproval of him.

When young Jim Bakker entered high school, things changed for the better for him. As he says in *Move that Mountain,* "I zoomed to the top of my class. . . . I was named editor of the school paper. . . . I also found I enjoyed talking before groups." And he became a popular disc jockey for school dances. "Most high school kids would sell their souls to be popular, and I was no exception."

But then, in the winter of 1958, while driving a 1952 two-toned blue Cadillac, he ran over a little boy, Jimmy Summerfield, and thought he had killed the child. "For the first time in my life, I surrendered to God. He was my only hope now."

The boy survived, and so did Jim's commitment. In 1959 he enrolled in North Central Bible College, in Minneapolis.

There, in his second year, he passed a girl in the hallway: "She was absolutely the cutest girl I had ever seen. She was wearing white socks, gym shoes, and a stiff purple crinoline skirt and looked to be less than five feet tall. . . . She was a little doll.

"She didn't wear a touch of makeup, so I nicknamed her 'my little holiness girl.'"

Tamara Faye LaValley was from the small papermill town of International Falls, Minnesota, where she was the eldest of eight brothers and sisters, growing up in an old two-story house. There was an outdoor toilet, and people took baths in galvanized tubs.

In *I Gotta Be Me,* Tammy wrote, "I thought our house was huge until I got married and discovered how little the house really was." When Jim took her to meet his parents, she was awed: "Their house had two bathrooms, big velvet drapes, curtains, a baby grand piano, and a kitchen with a dishwasher. I mean, their house had things I had never seen in my whole life."

There was fun in her childhood house, Tammy writes in *I Gotta Be Me,* although there was next to no money. On bath night, when the cleanest kids had to bathe first, since everyone shared the same water, her mother would also turn on the radio for the Saturday night "Barn Dance," and make a big pot of fudge—"the best fudge in the whole world!" And the kids were put to bed with their mother's songs as she rocked the cradle.

If her first visit to the Bakkers' house gave Tammy some surprises, Jim's first visit to Tammy's house presented him with some new experiences. Tammy describes the visit in *I Gotta Be Me:*

. . . Jim could not believe his eyes. It was like the Beverly Hillbillies. Four brothers and three sisters running up to him, kissing and meeting him. At this time we still didn't have a bathroom in the house.

All of my people are just nice American family people. Everybody got acquainted, we ate one of Mom's terrific snacks and soon we went to bed.

The next day Jim got up and wanted to take a bath. "Honey," he asked, "where's the bathtub?"

I brought two tubs to the bedroom and went to fill them with water. Jim looked at me so strange and asked, "What are these?" pointing to the tubs.

"Jim, we don't have a bathtub. That's what these are!"

The young Tammy had come early to music—her mother sang, and played the piano and guitar. Tammy remembers that in grade school she sang "Jesus Loves Me" with 100 of her schoolmates following her in a big, long line, singing too.

Tammy's brother Larry was also at PTL. A heavy-set short man who looked to be in his late thirties, he was in charge of the mechanic shop. I'd take a car over there for some particular repair we needed done right away, and he'd say, "We're closing now. Bring it back tomorrow." He didn't seem to know how to walk the extra mile. I started sending other people over there when it was necessary; I was tired of losing my temper.

Tammy and Jim never talked about him that I heard, but if Tammy saw him on the grounds, she'd go hug him, talk to him.

As far as I know, this was the only member of Tammy's family at PTL in 1984. Another brother was in jail that year, Tammy once said in the car. She was crying about him that day. I don't know where the rest of them were.

Actually, Tammy was full-blood kin only to her brother Donny; the younger six were her half-brothers and -sisters. Tammy's mother and father divorced when Tammy was very young. Rachel LaValley remarried, to a man named Fred Grover, when Tammy was six, a "wonderful man, whom I love dearly and was to me my daddy."

Fred Grover's car was an old Model A, and it embarrassed Tammy: "That car was just awful to me. . . . All the way home I would hope no one would see me."

The fact that Rachel had been divorced made her life in the Pentecostal church she attended difficult, and young Tammy took it to heart: "I was very young when I became aware that the church people were being mean to my mother. . . . I couldn't understand how they could take her money but wouldn't even let her play the piano . . . because she was divorced. To the church, my mother was just a harlot. . . . Mother continued to go, regardless of her heartache and hurt."

Still, ten-year-old Tammy went to the altar and received Christ into her heart. From then on she wanted to be an evangelist missionary.

Tammy liked speech class and being in the choir. As she entered her teens, however, her innocence and her deep religious beliefs were challenged in sometimes troubling ways.

Offered a part in a local production of the play *Oklahoma!*, she was excited, but "I had inner conflict over these plays because I had always been taught they were wrong. . . . Our church was a 'Can't Do Church.' You can't do this, and you can't do that! . . . I thought I was very brave to even be in the play at all. . . . The first time I wore makeup was in that play. I had been taught if you put on lipstick you are going to hell. That was it! How thankful I was that by now I had learned that God really loved me."

At fifteen, she thought that kissing a boy could make her pregnant, and was distressed that her boyfriend, although a Christian, still went to the movies.

Her second boyfriend, the pastor's son, became her fiancé when she had left high school and was working in Woolworth's. Ken was going to go to Bible college, but "for some unknown reason" didn't want her to go.

But Tammy felt "called by the Lord" to attend. With money her Aunt Gin had saved for her, she enrolled at North Central.

When Jim Bakker met Tammy LaValley, she was still engaged to the pastor's son. He wrote in *Move that Mountain:* "I'd occasionally see her in the hallways. And she would always wink at me. I thought to myself, 'That's not right for an engaged girl to do.' Little did I know that that was Tammy's way of being friendly and she was winking at a lot of other people, too."

Tammy and Jim began dating once she broke off her engagement, but not before she'd caused him more concern: "Each night Tammy would go ice skating with about five or six guys from the school. . . . They were all big brothers to her, but I was clearly irked by the situation."

I guess the tremendous jealousy he showed of Tammy while I was at PTL had been with Jim a long time.

They were married on April 1, 1961. ("We looked just like Barbie dolls in those [wedding] clothes," Tammy wrote in *I Gotta Be Me.*)

Jim says in *Move that Mountain,* "Since Tammy and I knew it was against North Central's rules to marry while attending school, we didn't bother going back to class. A few weeks [later] a letter arrived . . . we were no longer students at North Central."

But Jim and Tammy told me a different story about leaving North Central Bible College. They said it was because their religious beliefs were too radical for the college.

In the spring of 1984, North Central decided to give Jim an honorary doctorate. I was told that it would be the second honorary degree the college had ever given.

Jim was happy as could be about that, laughing and cheerful as we made plans to go to Minneapolis for the ceremony. Tammy was tickled too. They were both pleased.

North Central Bible College has had a long history of integrity, and its award to Jim was a very special event.

In 1987 I learned it wasn't true that Jim's was only the second honorary degree ever granted by the college, although it's true that the school has granted very few.

The degree was an Honorary Doctorate in Recognition of Life Achievement.

In 1987, the college president, Dr. Don Argue, said: "We feel—and our board feels—that we were desperately and despicably used."

In 1984, of course, Jim *looked* spotless. The college had no way of knowing what lay under the surface.

The people at the college were also unaware of the

Bakker spending spree that preceded and followed the ceremony.

We stayed at a big new downtown Minneapolis hotel, where the Bakkers and the kids had a suite; and David Taggart, Vi Azvedo, and I each had his own separate room.

The hotel was next to a multistory mall, and we shopped that for a day or two. I believe we went in every store in the mall. We spent a whole day in Dayton's, and we visited a *lot* of the other downtown stores too.

Tammy, I remember, bought eight or ten pairs of shoes, and a lot of jewelry—rings and necklaces. The stuff looked real to me, but it could have been fake. She liked cubic zircons, those fake diamonds, because she could get a lot more of them for the same money and she thought nobody could tell the difference.

Jim bought six suits, and about a thousand dollars worth of leisure clothing—summer jackets, summer shirts, white pants.

Tammy Sue got several outfits, and Jamie Charles some parachute pants.

David didn't buy much in Minneapolis; I don't think the things were elegant enough for him.

But David bought some stuff for me. In a store that was going out of business, he—I understood it wasn't he himself, but PTL and/or the Bakkers—gave me three suits. They were Whitehouse and Hardy, and cost sixty dollars apiece.

The gift created really mixed feelings in me. It seemed kindly. It seemed insulting, especially in view of the huge amounts they were spending on themselves. It seemed corrupting to accept it. It seemed okay to accept it. To work eighteen-hour days for seven months makes it okay to accept a $180 gift, doesn't it?

I took the suits, and said thank you. They were all pinstripes; David said pinstripes would give me a more authoritative look.

David was often generous toward people. He seemed to know when somebody had a need. At least five or six times he went out and bought a special-occasion dress for one or another of the women who worked for PTL. When he went out of town, he'd offer me the use of his Mercedes while he was gone. It wasn't just money-type things; he could always find time for the people who worked around the executives when they wanted to talk.

I received other gifts while I was at PTL, and maybe this is the place to tell about them.

The first was a birthday present from David and James Taggart in December. It was a Polo sweater, and it was beautiful. It was the most expensive sweater I'd ever owned.

The second was a bonus of $1000 in the summer of 1984. I'd been sharing a condo with a PTL singer who left without giving me his share of the month's rent. I was grousing about this around the place, because I was going to have to get out of the condo, and I liked the place.

David heard about this, and within a day or two handed me a PTL check for $1000.

"What's this for, David?" I asked. "How do I deserve this?"

"It's a bonus, Mike. Take it. It should cover the difference in rent for a couple of months."

I took it. I feel ashamed of taking it, still. It did cover half the rent up until I left PTL.

The trip back to Minneapolis was a triumphant return for the Bakkers. They'd come a long way from the penniless young newlyweds they'd once been.

After they left college, the young Jim and Tammy became traveling evangelists, and spent four years on the road before joining Pat Robertson's Christian Broadcasting Network in 1965. There they were to do a children's show—Tammy had discovered puppets—and a late-night talk show. In 1966 the talk show became *The 700 Club*.

Tammy loved to work puppets. She'd get behind the curtain, and the puppets would spring into life that she gave them, making them anybody she wanted to.

She was good at puppeteering, and I think it satisfied something very deep in her to disappear, be invisible. I sometimes thought her makeup was a mask, too. Something she could hide behind, the way she could hide behind the puppet curtain. Her singing seemed the same way to me. She could hide behind the song.

"Susie Moppet" and "Alley Alligator" were a great success on the Christian Broadcasting Network, but their meaning to Tammy Faye was deeper than simply their success.

She wrote, in *I Gotta Be Me*, "Many times because of our tiredness Jim and I would go on the show arguing about something. I would be so mad and disgusted with him and not even want to do the show. We still had to go on, smile and act happy for the children's sake. I'd get behind the curtain and Susie Moppet would be the one who would be terribly mad at Jim, and Alley would be the peacemaker. So it really worked for my personality; for Alley could talk Susie out of being mad, and by the time the show was over I wasn't mad at Jim anymore. I guess it was therapy for me."

Jim and Tammy left Pat Robertson in 1972 and entered television evangelism in California, but there was conflict with the board of directors and Jim resigned.

It was then the Bakkers came to Charlotte and started PTL, and eventually bought the land that became Heritage U.S.A.

It was in the early days in Charlotte that Jim kited checks, on the Lord's orders, according to *Move that Mountain:*

> Jim Thrash, the new general manager of WRET, . . . paid us a visit. "You owe us $70,000 in production costs," he announced grimly. . . . "I want the money within thirty days or I'm putting you off the air."
>
> It was impossible to come up with $70,000 in thirty days. We were only drawing $20,000 a month, and we had to pay salaries, equipment costs, building expenses, utilities, and a score of other bills with that.
>
> *"Give him what he asks,"* the Lord said, *"and I'll do the miracle for you."*
>
> The next Friday, I called Jim Moss into my office. "Have one of the girls in bookkeeping make

out a check for $20,000 and take it to Jim Thrash this afternoon."

His face flushed, "Jim, no way. We don't have it. Our deposits on Monday occasionally reach $7,000 but often less, and that's our big day."

"Write it and take it," I said.

. . . Thirty thousand dollars came in the mail. It was the greatest miracle of concentrated giving I'd ever witnessed—totally inspired by the Lord. . . .

The following Friday, the same thing happened. This time the check was for $20,000.

Maybe as an ex-cop I take too stern a view. But I call this writing bad checks.

But PTL was thriving. *Heritage Village Church* says that: "Only the Lord could have foreseen the ensuing growth, estimated by an expert at 7,000 percent within the next eighteen months. During that same period more than 100 new television stations began airing the broadcast; the staff doubled, then quadrupled; the first ever private satellite license was issued to PTL. . . . Hundreds of thousands of visitors came to Heritage Village [in Charlotte] and thousands of calls for prayer poured into the phone lines daily."

Jim proclaimed, on April 3, 1978, when dedicating PTL's satellite network, "We have begun a broadcast that will not stop until Jesus returns."

Indeed, it hasn't stopped yet.

CHAPTER 9

*Inasmuch as ye have done it unto one of the
least of these my brethren . . .*

MATTHEW 25:40

Both Jim and Tammy could be brutal to the
people under them.

Jim in particular had a way of wanting things done
immediately. When he gave an order, he wanted it
done right that instant, and he could be unreasonable. An example was the moving of his boat.

Jim's houseboat was about forty feet long and
twenty-five to thirty feet wide. It had two bedrooms
and a bathroom, a living room, and a kitchen. It was
just like a house, and had a television and air conditioning. It had a big deck all around, and another
deck on top of it. It was super.

The houseboat was out on the little (about two
acres) landlocked lake at Heritage U.S.A. Jim gave a
staff member orders to get the boat moved immediately.

It would have to be moved overland, sent to dry-
dock for repairs, and then the problem would be to

find a place on Lake Wylie where a boat that big could be put in the water.

It wasn't an overnight kind of job. In fact, the move took the better part of two months.

The guy nearly went crazy finding a firm that would undertake the move, and Jim's constant pressure was no help. At one point Jim told him that if the boat wasn't there the next day, he wouldn't have a job.

This was a man who had been with the ministry for years—a man who worked his heart out!

I couldn't believe it, because I thought Jim valued the man—but *he* could.

It was characteristic of Jim to threaten people, I'm sorry to say. But it did get things done.

Finally the moving of the houseboat was achieved, and it was put into Lake Wylie. Then another problem came up—quite literally.

The boat had been put in at the only place it could be, which was across the lake from Jim's house. Between the boat and the house was a bridge, the bridge that connects North and South Carolina on Highway 49—and the lake was too high for the boat to go under it.

Several days went by, and Jim was in an absolute uproar because the guy he'd told to do it couldn't get the boat to his house. Jim couldn't seem to accept the fact that the staffer couldn't make the water go down. Jim told him to call Duke Power and have them let water out of the lake so the boat could be taken under the bridge! He did what Jim told him. You can imagine what Duke Power said. It began something like "Listen, fella . . ." The man was patient and kept measuring until the day came.

The boat made it under the bridge with about one inch to spare.

When the boat reached the house, there was more pressure. Jim wanted the boat immaculately cleaned. About ten people had to be sent down from PTL to scrub it up.

Jim enjoyed the boat for a while, taking it out on Sunday afternoons. He much preferred it to his other boat, a ski-boat type speedboat. He didn't like the speedboat because it was a year or two old. So we went over to the lake marina, and Jim bought a brand-new boat for about $10,000.

I was hearing a lot of television talk about the ministry needing a lot of money to pay off bills, and there he was spending money on a second speedboat. I say "he"—David Taggart paid the bills. Where he got the money from, which bank accounts, I have no idea.

Jim's disturbing habit of turning conversations on and off, which I had observed in my first interview with him, was very much his daily way.

He'd pick up the radio in the car, bark orders at Jimmy Swain, who handled special projects—like Christmas City, for instance—then would immediately turn to something else.

People seemed to be dirt to him, dispensable, except for the few people who were close to him. Jimmy, Don Hardister, David Taggart, Vi Azvedo, Charlotte Whiting (the vice-president who was his "personal do-er"), Uncle Henry Harrison, maybe me, and a few others were not dispensable to him, maybe. The others, the workers, he just didn't seem to care about. Here today, gone tomorrow was fine with him. I remember a PTL singer who was fired because Tammy Faye simply didn't like him; he asked to see Jim and Tammy, and they saw him, but they fired him anyway.

Jim had a way of never telling you directly when you'd done something wrong. Instead, he'd tell David, or someone else, and expect him to deal with the problem.

When Jim had something he wanted kept secret—like the plans to a part of the hotel that he didn't want to get out yet—or something he felt was very private that he wanted to talk over with one of the vice-presidents, he would want me (and anybody else, too) to keep forty or fifty feet away. He wanted you to be right where he could see you, and make eye contact with you, but far enough away that you couldn't hear what he was talking about.

If we were walking around the hotel and I wasn't where he could see me, or if I should get behind a wall while we were walking, he would turn around and come looking for me. He really didn't like it if I was out of his sight, even for a minute. More than once he broke off in the middle of a conversation with somebody to come looking for me because I was out of view for a minute. He always wanted to know I was there. Whether we were in church on Sundays or he was giving a speech to thousands of people, he always wanted to be able to make immediate eye contact with me. Sometimes it made checking security really difficult.

When Jim was in a good mood in the morning, he'd

come out to the car with a smile on his face. But when he came out with a taut face and his jaw locked, I knew there was trouble. On this kind of morning, if he wasn't stony silent, he'd rattle off ten things that were wrong. Why hadn't the grass been cut? Why hadn't the trees been trimmed? Why hadn't the pool been cleaned? Why weren't the guards doing their job? Why didn't George have his breakfast ready? Had the dogs been fed? Where was David Taggart this morning? Where was Don Hardister? He'd rattle off a ton of critical questions like this. At times like this I noticed the whiskers behind his ears.

A lot of times I wouldn't say anything.

People who were around Jim a lot had to learn to sense when to talk to him and when not to. Most of the time he liked people to keep their mouths shut. Also, his questions often seemed to be just thinking out loud—at least, he didn't seem to expect any answer.

If he really wanted me to answer, he would usually repeat the question again, or he would look at me and say, "Well, what is your explanation for it?"

He'd expect me to have an answer, whether it was part of my job or not. He'd expect me to take care of it, too. It was always that way; Jim didn't want to bother with finding the person who was responsible for the thing he was asking about. He just demanded an answer of whoever was closest. And if he asked you a question, he wanted an answer that was short and to the point. No excuses, and no saying it wasn't your responsibility. He surely didn't like people to ask him questions.

I had to learn to read him on this, as on so much else. A lot of things were better left unsaid.

There were very few people he would speak directly to. If there was a problem with one of the maids in the house, he wouldn't speak to her. Instead he'd complain to me or George.

Same thing about Tammy Faye. She wouldn't speak directly to *anybody,* most of the time. What she would do is talk to Jim while I was with them in the car. She knew that I would hear what she said and that I would probably take care of whatever it was.

But she wouldn't speak directly to me about it.

In a way, Tammy was much harder on people than Jim. She'd take sudden dislikes to them, and demand that Jim fire them. Sometimes Jim would stand up for them and refuse to let them go; but he often went along with what she wanted.

At times the things Tammy complained about were simply not so. She'd say the floor hadn't been mopped, and I knew it had. Or she'd say the maid wasn't doing her job—she'd happened to walk into the kitchen before the maid washed the dishes.

One guard out at the house, Tammy said, was "looking" at her. She almost caused me to have to fire him. He was a married man in his mid-forties, and he had no interest in Tammy Faye. I managed to save the situation; I reassigned him away from the house for a while, and gradually worked him back in out there, telling him "Now, you just kind of stay away from her."

At PTL, people were often reassigned, or fired, with no idea of why it had happened.

In those cases they'd almost always innocently irritated one of the Bakkers in some way, or one of the other higher-ups. The first the employee knew of something being wrong, very often all he ever found out, was when he was moved or fired without any explanation.

It was management by personal whim all too often.

This meant that everybody was uneasy, a little off balance, all the time. You never knew where criticism would come from next—you were never quite sure whether you were pleasing Jim.

It made for a lot of tension.

Even with all the time I spent with Jim, it was David Taggart who'd tell me if there was something Jim didn't like about what I was doing. It rattled me.

As my first few weeks being Jim's bodyguard passed, I was really going short of rest. In December, when Jim would often want to go back to Heritage U.S.A. to admire Christmas City, I'd spend a lot of hours out at the house, in the guard shack, just waiting.

I must say Jim was bad about telling when he would want me again. He seldom said, "Take an hour, Mike," or anything like it. Sometimes, after I'd been with him all day, he'd call me at home at ten o'clock at night, and I'd have to go back and pick him up.

And the problem was the same in the daytime. He'd never tell me when he'd need me; he just expected me to be there. But in charge of the guards at the house, as I was, I had to find time to do that part of my job, too.

In his defense, Jim often didn't know when he'd need me again.

I began checking in with David Taggart to learn his schedule. But this system didn't work very well.

In the spring Jim was invited to the White House, to meet with Vice-President Bush. I was making preparations to go, when David told me Jim didn't want me to make the trip.

That was fine with me.

But the day Jim got back, he asked me, "Where were you?" As if I hadn't shown up for work. "Why didn't you come?"

Then Jim added the question that startled me: "Are you getting tired of me?"

I'd hear that again and again. Whenever I was absent, "Are you getting tired of me?"

It seemed a very odd question for your boss to ask.

I told him why I hadn't gone with him to Washington.

He said then, "From now on, every step I take, you take."

David seemed to enjoy keeping things stirred up between Jim and whoever might be getting close to Jim. He seemed to be uneasy about my getting along well with Jim, but Richard Dortch's arrival at PTL kind of made him relax about me. Took his attention off me, you might say.

David fielded a lot of Tammy Faye's complaints about service, too. Many times he'd slam down the phone after talking to her, trying to soothe her down, and yell, "Tammy Faye is a *bitch!*"

It was a big celebration when James Robison came to PTL to hold his crusade in July, and Jim was so happy to see him—but then Robison came back with Nelson Bunker Hunt, one of the fabulously wealthy Hunt brothers of Texas, and we gave them a full, detailed tour of the Heritage Grand Hotel. David said they were afraid Robison was trying to steal ideas from Jim, to get Hunt to back something very similar in Texas.

Jim said: "Why'd he bring Hunt if not to copy me? All they're doing is looking for my ideas."

Hunt was said to have given Robison some land.

Jim went on, "He's going to use my ideas to build a theme park in Texas."

Even though Jim showed them all around, all peaches and cream on the surface, he didn't trust Robison a bit.

On television, or when Jim was with the Partners, Jim would give all the credit to God for what he was doing, but in private it was always "What I have done . . . What I am going to do . . . My ideas. . . ." I don't think he fully believed that God deserved the credit. He was just at that point, I think, where he was bold enough to believe that he could do or get anything he wanted.

The people who lived and worked at PTL were almost every one very sincere, dedicated people. Jimmy Swain sticks in my mind from 1984 as a really good man, dedicated to the ministry, overworked to exhaustion. He didn't ask for extravagant gifts or high-style living. He was good to the Partners. He was good to the people there. His heart was just open to people, and he was dedicated to doing the right thing.

Jimmy was Head of Special Projects and General

Manager of Heritage U.S.A., and one of the main guys that kept PTL going. He gave so much of himself that it nearly destroyed his personal life.

I guess it was his inspiration, and Charlotte Whiting's too, that kept me around as long as I was.

The nice thing about PTL was the common people there, who lived there and worked there. They did their best to overlook things that seemed bad about the Bakkers.

A lot of them had left good-paying jobs, high-paying jobs, to come there, because they felt Jim had a destiny with God and they wanted to be a part of it. They had made big sacrifices, for their families as well as themselves, to do work for God. And here was Jim, having every possible thing that he could want so far as material goods were concerned. Yet they seemed not to pay any attention to what he said or what he did, except for the good things. They just did their work.

Tammy Sue and Jamie Charles attended Heritage Academy, the school on the grounds, and certainly those two kids had all the clothes and things any kid could want—and yet, if any of the parents felt any resentment on their kids' behalf, I never heard of it.

They just overlooked the bad things.

If Jim came into a room where ordinary people were working, they'd say, "Hallelujah! Here's Jim!" and rise to their feet, smiling, and sometimes they'd clap for him.

Sometimes they'd reach out, just to touch his arm, with so much love in their faces.

The Partners did that, too, when they came to visit.

They all really thought Jim Bakker was a great man.

David Taggart and Richard Dortch both had a way of talking about "niggers" that I didn't like. It seemed racist to me.

Jim and Tammy never used the word, that I remember. But it was true that black people were very much in the minority at PTL.

And Penny Hollenbeck was criticized because she had a black friend, one of the male PTL singers. There was gossip about them, unfounded. She was friends with the singer's whole family.

She was eventually fired. It was hard for me to swallow that. She did a super job, and she was an innocent young girl.

Gossip and back-stabbing were unfortunately a way of life in the higher reaches of PTL.

And fear.

I was totally loyal to Don Hardister. But as I made a success of being with Jim, Don seemed to grow cool to me. I thought he wasn't altogether pleased that I was managing to please this extremely difficult man. After all, only one person had been with him on a daily basis before me.

And yet Don had been with the ministry so long. I felt he shouldn't have felt uneasy about me, or feared that I might displace him somehow.

It was just the way things were at the high levels of PTL.

Fear.

Fortunately, I think I was able to show Don that

my loyalty was to him, and as far as I was concerned we resumed and strengthened our friendship.

I didn't blame Don.

You never knew when Jim might decide you'd joined the dispensables.

And yet, I remember him being nice to me when I deserved for him to be mean to me, or at least angry at me.

Once, for instance, Jimmy Swain and I had gone out to Mulberry Village with him in Jimmy's four-wheel-drive Jeep, to prospect around the back wooded area.

We arrived at the place where Jim wanted to stop. He and Jimmy got out to walk, and Jimmy called back over his shoulder, "Mike, you bring the Jeep on up after us."

Well. There was a little creek right there at the foot of the hill. It looked all right for the Jeep, but when I was halfway across it, that Jeep just sank right into the mud.

I couldn't budge it.

I trudged up the hill feeling foolish. How could I have been so stupid? I also thought, *this* is why Swain wanted me to drive the Jeep up here. He knew the Jeep would get stuck, and he wanted somebody else to do it! He loved pulling pranks like that, playing jokes on people. Next time it'd be my turn, but right then I had too much egg on my face to think much about getting him back.

I was sure I was in for a bawling out. I'd seen Jim do mean things to people for less than that.

As I approached, they turned around and saw me, and looked back to see were the Jeep was. I looked at Jimmy Swain, trying to ignore Jim. I could see the gleam in Jimmy's eye.

"Jimmy," I said to Swain. "Listen, we've got a problem."

Swain looked at me and grinned. "What's the problem?"

"You know that little green Jeep you have that's supposed to go through anything? It's sitting back there stuck in the mud."

Jim looked at Jimmy and said, "Yeah, Jim, we bought that thing because we were supposed to go anywhere on the property in it."

Jimmy said, "It must be the driver, not the Jeep."

They both started laughing.

Jim looked at me, still smiling, and said, "Go ahead and get the Jeep out of the mud. I guess I'll just have to depend on Jimmy to protect me for the next few minutes until you get it out."

I went back down and radioed to Maintenance. They sent a tractor over to pull us out.

Meanwhile Jim and Jimmy had walked on out to the road.

I drove to where we'd left Jim's car, parked the Jeep, took Jim's car, and caught them down on the road.

They didn't say anything about what had happened—and I sure didn't, either.

And I remember one particular day when we were shooting the show down by the rotunda, near the just-begun Water Park. After the show Jim was addressing the audience, and I guess his remarks went on a little too long to suit me. I was bored.

Near me was a scaffold, just the right height for

doing chin-ups. I began chinning myself. One-arm chin-ups, just to keep myself amused.

Then I heard applause. I looked around and the entire audience had turned and was watching me, clapping! Jim was watching me, too. I wanted to sink into the ground.

Jim caught my eye, shook his head, and grinned.

He never fussed at me for that, either—even though I certainly deserved it. I'd messed up his work.

I saw him be mean to other people, but he just never was to me.

For me to sit here and say that the Bakkers didn't do a lot of good things would be wrong. They did. They helped a lot of people. They helped missions. They gave $100,000 to the Good Will to build another wing on their building in Charlotte, and they helped a lot of individuals. Jim gave one of his cars to an evangelist who was running some seminars at PTL. Evidently he was having some financial difficulties at the time. Jim made a generous donation to North Central Bible College around the time I arrived at PTL. It was one of the truly nice things he did, I thought, to give to a school that had dismissed him. It was in the thousands of dollars. It was going toward something they were building, I think.

They had about seven hundred PTL drop-off points across the country, mostly people's homes, where the needy could go for food and clothing. (In 1986, PTL claimed over a thousand.)

They opened the PTL Home, so that pregnant girls could come in and have their children without having an abortion.

They had a prison ministry.

The heart of the prison ministry program was to give prisons satellite dishes, so that the inmates could watch Christian programming. Donations were solicited, and came in, and then they'd have to get the prison's permission to install the dish. They did place several while I was there.

Tammy Faye went to one or two women's state prisons while I was there. Vi Azvedo accompanied her on a trip down to one in Georgia, I remember.

She took a PTL film crew along, and later they had a TV special on it.

On Wednesdays and Sundays PTL volunteers visited county jails in the area, and I believe there was a program of visits on a daily basis, as well.

In 1986 PTL said it had over 8000 volunteers, reaching into more than 1000 jails in America and fourteen foreign countries, and said it distributed over 25,000 Bibles to prisoners each year.

A PTL home for the homeless was in the planning stage. After I left, it came into being. It's called Fort Hope.

To say that they didn't do a lot of good things would be absolutely wrong, because they did. But still, their good deeds didn't outshadow, to me, the bad things that they were doing, the way they were wasting money and the way they were treating people around them. I didn't agree with the way they were running the ministry.

I always had the philosophy that if you can't back the boss that feeds you, then definitely don't cut his hand off, get out. By June I had seen enough, and had settled within myself that I had taken all that I could take. I just didn't feel that they were doing the right thing.

I knew it was time for me to start looking for another job.

Still, some days I admired Jim for the things that he did and for his courage, and some days I admired Tammy Faye's sweetness and seeming concern for other people.

Both Jim and Tammy had problems of their own, and they really had to struggle with them.

Some days Jim couldn't even leave the house. He'd spend a whole day in bed, only coming out once or twice to eat. He'd had ulcers, years before, and he had a nervous breakdown in 1969 when he couldn't leave his house for a month. He'd had a horrible time, according to *Move that Mountain:* "It seemed as if whatever little control I had over myself might snap at any minute, and I'd be floating in an emotional stream unable to return."

He couldn't sleep for longer than five minutes, and if he took a shower the water felt like hundreds of tiny needles.

He'd recovered through rest, recreation, and adoption of a healthier diet—but this kind of difficulty lay in wait for him even in 1984.

One day in the dressing room after the show, he just collapsed. He'd been having a meeting in there. When the people had left, Vi Azvedo came out to me, saying, "Jim's sick. He's overtired."

When we went in he was lying on the couch, shivering.

"I can't get warm," he said.

He was acting like a man with a very high fever,

almost out of his mind. I found a blanket, and Vi and I draped it around his shoulders and helped him out to the car.

He lay in the backseat, his head in Vi's lap.

We got him home and put him to bed.

He stayed there for a day or two, resting.

He frequently became exhausted. He would just go and go and go and go until it seemed almost inhuman, what he put himself through. Trying to make sure that he collected all the money he needed for PTL, and worrying about every little light bulb on the place, every little squiggle in the blueprints.

One thing Jim liked about me was that I didn't get excited. No matter what the situation, Jim knew I had it under control, and that made him feel comfortable. He didn't like people around him who got excited or nervous. If somebody got really nervous around Jim, it would make him nervous, until you'd almost think he was having a nervous breakdown.

Sometimes Jim went to the chiropractor. "Having my bones cracked takes all my tension out," he'd say. And every now and then he'd call one or another PTL person in to give him massages.

But mostly he'd take to his bedroom for a day or two when he just couldn't handle things. It might be two days in one week, or one day in two or three weeks. There was no set pattern.

With some frequency he'd tell me to call this or that PTL person to come over to the dressing room behind the studio and give him a massage.

I'd make the call, and the man would come over to the dressing room. He and Jim would go into the workout area where the massage table was and lock the door behind them.

Sometimes the massages were extremely brief, and those sessions don't stick in my mind particularly.

But some of the massage sessions lasted an hour and a half.

At the end of that time, the PTL employee of the day would then open the door to the workout area and say something like, "Let him sleep for an hour or so."

The men who had given these long massages would then be unusually talkative, chatting away about anything but having just given Jim a massage. Their sleeves were usually rolled up, and their faces were usually flushed.

The circumstances of the extended massage sessions had an uneasy feeling for me. They just didn't feel right at all.

I didn't know what was going on in there. I still don't. I just knew that I didn't like sitting out there on the other side of the door at those times.

As I thought about it then, I'd wonder why he never asked me to give him a massage. I wasn't a masseur, true. But neither were any of the men he had leave their work to come massage him!

These long hours in the massage room just plain didn't sit right with me.

In early August 1987, *Time* magazine reported:

"A former close aide to Bakker . . . told *Time* that he had a homosexual relationship with Bakker from 1983 until last November. . . . The man says the intimate sessions sometimes occurred in Bakker's posh studio office after the show."

Jim has denied this report.

In 1984, I was ignorant of what was going on in there, and I still am.

All I know is what I felt about sitting out there.

Time Magazine also reports that a second PTL person had a shocking encounter with Jim at the Tega Cay house: "Bakker had asked the aide to give him a massage. As the aide performed that service, he claims, Bakker made an explicit sexual pass. 'I froze and staggered off toward the door,' the man says, adding that Bakker called him last April and accused him of disclosing the incident to televangelist Jerry Falwell.

" 'He said, "I'll put my hand on a stack of Bibles and swear you touched me first," ' the aide says."

Jim has denied this as well.

There were a *lot* of days Jim took to his bedroom, and I stayed on duty outside. It was very common for him to call this PTL person or that over for a conference in there. He'd take to his bed for a day or two whenever he felt he just couldn't face the world. It might be two days in one week, or one day in two or three weeks. There was no set pattern.

Jim was an amazingly insecure person. Something that may seem odd, in view of what I've just been writing about, but something that is nevertheless true, is that Jim often didn't want to go home in the afternoon unless Tammy was home. Sometimes we'd ride around the grounds for an hour or more, waiting for word that she'd come home.

If Jim was insecure, so was Tammy. I don't think she believed people could like her.

She and Jim *did* spend a lot of time in the bedroom, as I've mentioned before. I have no idea what went on in there. But I know that I did not have the feeling that they were rushing in there to make love.

It seemed to me their bedroom was rather, or as well, their refuge from the world.

Whatever the case, Tammy was more suspicious of people than Jim was, less willing to trust people.

In *I Gotta Be Me,* she wrote: "The very first thoughts that come into my heart when new people come into our organization are, 'Is that the one? Is he going to try to take over now?' . . . .

"I never know who is my real friend. This is one of the problems of being well-known. . . .

"Nobody knows what it's like to be in the limelight, unless they have been there themselves. I know how much one wants to be a person just like everyone else, and not be set on a pedestal, and not have to live up to something all the time that you really aren't."

Tammy had also had a terrible time with her health, after the birth of her daughter Tammy Sue. In the hospital, she wrote, "I had to have nurses with me throughout the first night because I saw spiders crawling all over the drapes and I tried to jump out of bed to kill them. I had mice under my bed and was trying to kill them too. . . . It was like I was having a bad drug trip. The third day I finally realized I had a baby. . . ."

Two weeks later, "I was beginning to get nervous. I would sit on the couch and shake from the effect of drugs and lack of sleep. I was being given too much medication. I didn't know what to do or how to handle it. . . .

"Suddenly I couldn't pray anymore. I couldn't cry anymore. I couldn't laugh anymore, and I couldn't even let Jim touch me. . . . I thought I was crazy. . . .

"The nurses later told me that they had given me an almost fatal overdose of medication."

At last she was able to pray again, and was able to agree to sing at a revival meeting. "The Holy Spirit freed me that night. As I ministered, I felt the Holy Spirit as I hadn't in months." But she had been through a year of "such unspeakable torment that I thought I was going to die."

Considering their problems, I really did admire the nice things Jim and Tammy were able to do.

Jim was so nice to Brad Lacey, for instance. Brad, a Charlotte newscaster, had had a crippling heart attack. Jim, knowing Brad couldn't work too hard, hired him as a public relations man. Brad was just happy to be alive, determined to make every day cheerful, and he did. That hot summer of '84, he had the Billy Graham Home as his special project, and he was forever taking visitors on tours of it. (Several times invitations were sent to Billy Graham for him to come see the Home, but he never did while I was there.) Then Brad had another heart attack—and it killed him.

That night I took Jim and Tammy over to Mrs. Lacey's house, and they stayed until the wee hours.

Jim did the funeral service. It was in the studio— not for publicity, but because that's where Brad would have wanted it. A lot of the Charlotte news people came. I remember looking over at newscaster Bill Walker—who gave me a smile—and thinking it was a day of truce. The press was there for Brad, not to attack Jim.

Jim's eulogy was the best I've ever heard, and the service was the most comforting funeral I've ever attended. He said, "When you look at the Billy Graham Home, you'll think of Brad Lacey. He'll always be here. When you see a tram car full of people, Brad will be there swinging on the side of the car, telling them all about things. When you come on these grounds feeling bad or feeling down, remember Brad Lacey is here somewhere; you just can't find him right now."

Jim made it easier for all of us to let Brad go, because he made us see that we *weren't* really letting him go. We still had him. Jim spoke directly to Mrs. Lacey and the children—four or five, all grown—in a way that really comforted them. He helped Mrs. Lacey, and all the rest of us, that day.

Some days, like that one, I would think that maybe I dreamed up all of the bad stuff I was seeing. I would think that maybe it was just me. Days would go by when Jim was so nice to people, and he would talk so kindly about them—but then suddenly he'd go off on the other end.

Sitting here writing about it, I'm still troubled. I'd say to myself, "The good things have got to outweigh the bad. They've got to. So let's overlook the bad and just say that they are doing the right thing."

And they could justify anything. Jim would say, "Christians deserve the best of everything." His message was, Hey, you can have everything you want.

And money is nothing. God is everything, but money is nothing. So send me all your money and let me spend it. God will take care of you. That was kind of the philosophy he preached.

But money was a lot more than nothing to him, because he needed money to supply all of these habits that he had, the extravagant life-style. I mean, he and Tammy lived in an absolute fantasy world.

But the way he treated the people who came to help build the hotel took the cake.

Jim got on the television pleading for people to come work on the hotel. He had to have good carpenters, he said, and he didn't care where they came from. There was food, shelter, good jobs, he said, good-paying jobs.

Roe Messner had put the work on slowdown, because he was falling far behind in getting paid by PTL. He said to me, "I can't believe that he is asking people to come out here and work. I don't know how I am going to pay the people I have now."

But these people were showing up. I remember one couple that I talked to. They had come from Texas. The man and his wife hadn't had that much to start with, but they had heard the television plea, and they believed so much in Jim and Tammy Bakker that he just quit his job and they loaded up their stuff in the truck and came. When they get to PTL, there are no openings. So he is stuck without any money. So what does he do? He doesn't have the money to get back home. He doesn't have *anything*.

He wanted to talk to Jim, but Jim wouldn't see him. I talked to him for about an hour. This guy was standing there crying like a little baby and telling me what he and his wife had been through.

I asked him, "Have you talked to anybody else who has been through this same thing?"

He said, "Yes. There are a lot of us like this. Jim said, 'Lay down whatever you are doing and come on over here.' And then when we get here, we find out that PTL is not doing the hiring and that Roe Messner's company is, except that he is not hiring anybody. He doesn't have room for anybody."

This guy was heartbroken. After he left I had to go somewhere private and just break down.

I would love to know where the guy is today. Did he even survive? He believed so much in PTL, and he believed so much in the Bakkers. Everything they said was the gospel to him. And now, to be ruthlessly thrown out into the world like this . . .

It breaks my heart to think about him.

He wasn't the only one. I personally spoke to about twenty couples who wanted to see Jim. I couldn't help them; I didn't have the money. As far as I know, PTL didn't do anything for any of these people.

I wanted to take Jim and shake him, and say: "Hey, look at what's going on. Look at what you are doing to little people, man. You're destroying them. The people that you tell to come here and do the things that you want done, the people who have actually put you where you are.

"And here you are building a rich man's world, and a hotel nobody can afford to come to except the rich. These people don't have a hundred dollars a night, or sixty dollars or fifty dollars a night. They're making ten thousand or fifteen thousand a year and trying to raise a family and hardly have a car that will get here!

"You know they believe you, Jim. You know they believe you because you can sell anything. They get here, and all of a sudden their dream crashes!

"God knows you need a bodyguard. You really need a bodyguard. Because some of these people are going to go absolutely off the deep end one day, because you are misleading them."

I hated myself. I really did.

Not that I'm such a great person. It just didn't take a saint to see that this was wrong. The thing that disturbed me so much was that Jim didn't see it. Or if he did see it, he didn't let on. It seemed very clear that these people didn't mean anything to him.

None of these people got to talk to him. My orders were to keep them away from him. And not only the people who'd come to work on the hotel.

Folks would drive thousands of miles to see the show live, and they figured they'd get to see him and talk to him when they were there. He'd say a few words to them in the studio after the show, but that was it. They'd want to see him in private. They'd find out I was his bodyguard, and they'd hand me notes to give him, to please pray for this or pray for that, or please make time to talk to them. I gave Jim the notes a couple of times, and that was a drastic error. David told me never to give Jim any more notes because they upset him. Can you imagine? His people's notes upset him. So I was to give all notes to David, and none to Jim.

I talked to numerous old folks there, who said that

they only had $300 or $400 a month Social Security and they sent him forty or fifty dollars a month. I met plenty of people like this—and he wouldn't see them! It was absolutely more than I could handle.

CHAPTER 10

Whilst we are at home in the body . . .
II CORINTHIANS 5:6

Home for Jim and Tammy Faye was in Tega Cay, about ten or twelve miles from PTL, a residential community on the shore of Lake Wylie, a dammed lake that, while public, belonged to Duke Power Company.

Once we had entered Tega Cay, that first day I took Jim home, we drove all the way through to the lake area and up a hill. At the top of the hill was a gate, and a television camera. The guard watching the monitor down at the house recognized the car and opened the gate for us. Then down a steep hill to the house on the edge of the lake.

Jim got out of the car and darted into the house. He moved like lightning when he had a mind to.

Immediately the guards came and took the car and started washing it. They washed and vacuumed it every day, getting it ready for the next morning.

The house was big. Its exterior seemed almost Japanese, with its stained wood siding and high points to the roof. An Oriental castle. The trees and flowers had a manicured look.

This, of course, is the house that was much fought over in 1987, with the Bakkers claiming they owned it and PTL claiming it owned it. This is where the air-conditioned doghouse was that the press wrote about in 1987—but it wasn't built until after I left.

When we went to Palm Desert, to the house out there, I can still see Tammy throwing her arms wide, saying, "I'm *so* glad we bought this house! This is the first house we've gotten to be our very own—the first that's really ours."

Whoever owned the house at Tega Cay, it was home to the Bakker family. Jim was thinking, though, of building a house at Heritage U.S.A., in an area called Lake Park Place that he planned to develop in "truly unique homes" beginning at 2000 square feet.

The Tega Cay house was put on the market very discreetly that spring, with an asking price of $1.4 million, being offered through a realtor in nearby River Hills. Nobody wanted to buy it, and it was taken back off the market. The house at Lake Park Place never got built, either.

Jim and I visited the Lake Park Place site. He was planning a very big house, kind of tucked into a lake-front bank. He described it to me in great detail, as if he could see it there instead of the trees and under-growth, then seemed to focus directly on me.

"Why don't we put a small apartment in it for you, Mike? You know I like having Security around, and it would save you a lot of off-grounds expense."

It was kind for him to offer this, but I shuddered at

the thought. All I could think of was that there I'd have no private life at all. I had little enough as it was. I thanked him and said no.

The house had fifteen or sixteen rooms—the best I was able to count them—and it had three main entrances. There was a door from the two-car garage into the house, a front door that opened into an entrance hall in front of the living room, and then the kitchen door, which was down a few steps from the parking area. The house was built on a steep slope above the lake, and the driveway side was some twenty or thirty feet above the lakeside.

When I began working there, the kitchen was done in a country style, but in the spring they redecorated in what they called "French country." The kitchen was about fifteen by twenty, with wood cabinets and a double window over the sink. It had super equipment, including a dishwasher, two ovens, and a microwave.

A wood-paneled area right off the kitchen was set up like a little den, furnished with a couch and a chair, a round table, a television set, and some bookshelves. This was the usual family sitting area.

If you could call it that. The Bakkers didn't spend time together as a family. Usually when I brought Jim home in the evening, he'd go right into the bedroom, then come out after a while and say, "Tammy Faye will be down in a few minutes." She'd come out, and we'd go out to eat. When the kids didn't come with us, a maid or two would stay and feed them. When the kids were coming with us, David Taggart would call ahead to the house and tell the maids to get them ready.

Right off the den area was a breakfast nook, also wood paneled, with an oak table and chairs. It had lots of windows, and opened onto a patio that over-looked the lake. You could see the den television from here. This was where the family ate their meals, as a rule, when they ate at home.

If you came back into the kitchen and went to the left, there was a wallpapered, formal dining room with a large white dining table and high-backed, white-upholstered chairs. The room had a lot of plants, including small trees, which did well there, for the dining room had a glass roof. It was super nice, but it was *very* seldom used. Guests were usu-ally fed in restaurants; but if, as occasionally hap-pened, they were to eat at the house, the meal was served in the breakfast nook.

If you came back into the kitchen, next you could enter a hallway that was used for storage. Off to its right was a large pantry stocked with food, just thou-sands of dollars worth of food.

George, the guard in charge inside the house, was in charge of groceries, and he and Vi would often make the grocery list, following what they under-stood of Tammy Faye's general guidelines.

Tammy liked having vast quantities of food in the house.

Beyond the pantry was the atrium, about twenty by twenty, which was a kind of three-sided green-house. It had plants upon plants; and six to ten tropi-cal birds, parrots, cockatoos, lived there in cages.

George was told to clean the bird cages every day. He did it faithfully, but Tammy would complain frequently that he didn't. Poor George. He had more grief over those cages.

The Bakkers never used the atrium.

As a girl, Tammy had been proud that her grandmother kept a parrot and "hundreds" of parakeets and canaries, which were sold to pet stores. She'd liked it that her school class was taken to visit them.

Maybe that's why she had the idea she wanted birds—but I never saw her get any enjoyment from them.

Continuing down the hallway and taking a step up, you passed a bathroom on the right and you were in the large, stone-floored entrance foyer behind the front door. Then there was the living room.

It was a big room, with lots of windows on the far wall overlooking the lake. They had white couches at the beginning, but changed the furniture while I was there, putting in floral couches. One wall was bookshelves, but they didn't read much that I saw, except for magazines. Jim liked *Newsweek, U.S. News and World Report, Entrepeneur,* and *Money.* Tammy subscribed to *Woman's Day, Redbook, House & Garden, Southern Living,* and *Glamour.* The remaining walls were light-colored and covered with pictures. They had statuettes everywhere, and animal sculptures—things that they had bought on their travels. There was a large-screen Mitsubishi television here.

Straight on through the living room was another hallway that led to the master bedroom. They enlarged the master bedroom while I was there, adding French doors and a deck that overlooked the lake. It had a light-colored carpet, a couch, some tables, another wide-screen TV, and a king-sized bed with a high, padded white headboard. They had the biggest down comforter I'd ever seen. It was white, too. They kept a lot of dried flower arrangements there, and there were some of Tammy Faye's dolls, and more animal ornaments.

Their dressing rooms had two separate entrances from the bedroom, but they met around at the back, and there was a large tub that you had to step up to. The tub area was full of plants.

Tammy's dressing room was about thirty feet long. All along one side, it was nothing but clothes, *hundreds* of dresses and outfits, hung that whole way. (I don't think I ever saw her wear the same outfit twice.) Her shoes, hundreds of pairs of them, were on racks under the hanging things.

On the other wall she had a couch and chair, both in pale colors, and a big dressing table area with mirrors all around it. Her half-dozen wigs, all of them close to the color of her own hair, most of them shoulder length, stood there on wig stands. And on this side were lots of drawers for storage.

Tammy's dressing room, like Jim's, had a toilet enclosure.

Jim's dressing room was considerably smaller, more like a walk-in closet, but there were lots of clothes in it: a hundred or so shirts, maybe forty suits, fifty to sixty pairs of trousers, twenty to thirty sport coats, two hundred ties, fifty pairs of shoes.

Jim wore loafers, lace-ups, or short zipper boot-style shoes. His shoes looked a lot like David's, which wasn't surprising, since he relied on David's taste in clothes.

Jim liked cowboy boots, too, and if we were going

to check on construction projects after the show, he'd often change into boots and jeans. Calvin Klein jeans. He liked Calvin Klein clothes a lot. He'd put on a pullover sweater and a down jacket to complete the outfit.

Jim wore very little jewelry other than his wedding ring. He had two watches. Both were gold. One had a leather band, and one had a gold band.

He had a small dressing table in his dressing room, and there was a shower enclosure in there, too.

Coming back out of the bedroom and into the hallway, you came to the stairs leading down. The walls were lined with pictures of Jim and Tammy with this or that notable person they'd met on their travels, and pictures of them and the kids.

Going down one floor, you entered another large living room, which I never saw them use. Off of that was Jim's study. It was book-lined, with big windows overlooking the lake, and furnished with a large desk and a high-back brown leather chair. He didn't spend much time there.

Then there was a workout room.

There was also a room that was a kind of entertainment center, with low seating, a large-screen TV, and a magnificent stereo system. The kids used this room a lot, I think, but Jim and Tammy didn't.

Beneath this was yet another floor, where there was a guest bedroom, and a playroom, and the kids' rooms.

Tammy Sue's room had twin beds with silvery bedspreads. She had a dressing room, too. She wasn't the neatest fourteen-year-old in the world: her room was usually covered with clothes.

There was a lot of tension between Tammy Faye and Tammy Sue. Tammy Faye was jealous of her fourteen-year-old daughter, I thought. Tammy Sue was beautiful, and she was super close to Jim. They had so many traits in common. They were both strong-willed, and neither one of them knew the meaning of the word *no*. Jim loved Tammy Sue deeply. Often, when we were in the car, he would tell her that someday she would be running the organization.

If Tammy Faye was with us, she didn't like Tammy Sue to talk to Jim. She'd interrupt constantly. I think Tammy Faye wanted Jim's attention for herself—on *her* problems, *her* demands.

Tammy Sue sometimes criticized her mother's clothes. Tammy Faye would shoot right back with criticism of her daughter's appearance, because Tammy Sue liked to wear tight jeans and clothes that were just too grown-up for her. They'd face off and go all stiff and shout at each other. It sounded more like two teenage girls fighting than it sounded like mother and daughter. Tammy Sue never changed her clothes after one of these fights, not that I saw.

Tammy Sue and Tammy Faye also fought a lot over how much freedom and independence Tammy Sue could have—whether she could be out on the PTL grounds late at night, or whether she could attend this or that party.

"I *hate* my mother!" Tammy Sue would say after losing yet another round. Unlike the clothes fights, Tammy Sue did lose these, sometimes.

Tammy Sue went to her father when she wanted

something, and she always got it. Jim just couldn't seem to say no to her.

There was a spate of car buying in the early spring, kind of a warm-up for the Rolls and the Mercedes they bought in California a couple of months later—and Tammy Sue profited from this one.

It started because Tammy Faye didn't like the white Chevrolet station wagon that was used primarily to carry the kids around, back and forth to school. She told Jim she was tired of it, and Jim told me to go find another one, but not white this time.

I went up to Charlotte and brought one back for them to see. It was a Pontiac station wagon, grayish green, and listed at $16,000. They liked it. I told David, and he sent the check up there. The white station wagon was turned over to the Security Department, and Don told me to take it and use it to get back and forth to the house. If they needed it on property, I'd hand it over to them.

Two days later, by the way, Tammy Faye was complaining that she didn't like the color of the new Pontiac.

Maybe because of the new station wagon, or maybe not, Jim decided he wanted a convertible. (I should have told you earlier: at this time Jim was using a navy Buick Park Avenue and Tammy had a white Buick Riviera. Both cars were said to have been donated by somebody in Ohio. That would explain why they had Ohio tags the first year, but not why the tags were illegally renewed in Ohio while I was there.)

Jim and I went to the Chrysler dealer not far from PTL, and he picked out a red Dodge convertible, a little four-cylinder car, about $14,000. So I called David, who got the check ready, and I picked the car up the very same day.

As the weather warmed up, he'd want to use this car, and we'd take it over to the property.

One day after the show I came down to the garage after the show, and it was *gone.* For a minute there, it was pure panic for me.

Tammy Sue had taken it.

Her guard said she'd just insisted.

Jim didn't fuss at her for doing this, as far as I know. There were always other cars around that he could commandeer.

The trouble with Tammy Sue and the convertible worsened. Her guards told me she was insisting on driving it around Heritage U.S.A. Tammy Sue was fourteen or fifteen (I forget when her birthday comes), and she had no license—not even a learner's permit. And no insurance, which is also required by South Carolina law.

I went to Jim about this. It really worried me. There were so many visitors on the grounds, so many people with their eyes shut, praying in the twisty road, that I was afraid of a tragic accident.

Jim seemed to think she could do anything she liked at Heritage U.S.A. That this was his property. He never did stop her from driving there.

And in fact Tammy Sue was very lucky. She never had an accident while I was there.

It became accepted that the convertible was Tammy Sue's.

Tammy Sue didn't like being with a guard all the time. She wanted more freedom. On that, Jim was firm. She was to be guarded at all times. Threats against her came in with some regularity, and at least one had been really scary, although nothing came of it.

Once, in Charlotte, at a party, she gave her guard the slip. The guard nearly went out of her mind before she found her again—sitting in one of the cars with a friend. I believe Jim never heard about that.

I discussed the incident with Vi Azvedo, and she promised me that she would talk to Tammy Sue, and make the girl see that ducking her guard was not funny.

Vi spent a great deal of time at the Bakker house. As well as helping with problems about Tammy Sue, she was Jim and Tammy Faye's personal counselor, you might say. She'd try to jolly them out of their bad moods, she'd work to smooth over Tammy's rages at Jim, and she'd generally try to keep their marriage running smoothly. She flattered them a lot, told them how much good they'd done in making the PTL ministry, and told them they deserved the good things of life. I didn't hear her raise her voice against their wild spending. On the contrary, I think she felt it was worth it if it made them happy.

I never saw Tammy Faye go anywhere with Tammy Sue, or with Jamie Charles, unless Jim was along.

Jamie Charles's room down on the bottom floor was smaller than Tammy Sue's. He had bunk beds. He usually kept it pretty tidy, but there'd be a few toys scattered around.

Jamie Charles was a cute little eight-year-old. He could have anything material he wanted. He asked for a tree house once, and Jim gave the order. Well, it ended up having two stories, standing on piers on a slope, eight-foot piers on the uphill side, twenty-foot piers on the downhill, with air conditioning and television. It had to cost $20,000; it was nicer than houses many people live in.

Jamie loved G.I. Joe, and he loved to hear me tell about being in the Marines. Like most eight-year-old boys, he really loved anything military.

He spent a lot of time out in the guard shack. We'd all play with him when we had time; that's what he wanted. If he got mad at a guard, even a man old enough to be his grandfather, he'd point his finger at him and yell, "You're fired! My daddy said I could fire you!"

The guys would come to me, really worried for their jobs at the hands of a child. I spoke to Jim about it, hoping he'd put a stop to it. He just grinned, and said, "He gets that manner from me." He looked pleased and proud.

I don't think Jim said anything to Jamie Charles; Jamie surely *never* stopped "firing" people while I was at PTL.

He didn't "fire" Carlos, though. Carlos was his favorite. A big, happy-go-lucky guy in his early twenties, Carlos would take Jamie down to the dock, spend hours showing him how to fish, and take him out to explore the woods—kind of teaching him the things boys want to learn. Carlos's car was a hot black Camaro, and Jamie loved to ride in it.

Jamie really loved Carlos.

Jamie Charles would get "sick" in Sunday school pretty often, and come over to Jim and Tammy's dressing area behind the Barn. Since Jim and Tammy were in services in the Barn, I'd go see to him. He'd ask me for candy, and for stories. He hated it when I told him I had to go back to the services. He always hated people leaving him.

I felt sorry for Jamie. Nobody was looking after that child the way a boy that young needs looking after.

Sometimes on the road, when I would be living with them, and sometimes when we were in Tega Cay, too, I ended up putting Jamie Charles to bed, even when Tammy and Jim were home. When we came back from dinner, there would often be no "good nights." I'd be getting the kids, and often Vi Azvedo, out of the car, and Jim and Tammy would just enter the house and be gone into the bedroom by the time we came inside. I felt bad about that. I think an eight-year-old needs his mother to put him to bed. A parent, anyway.

In Palm Desert one day, when Tammy Faye seemed very much herself, she said she was worried about Jamie Charles, that he was so far from his play-mates and might be lonesome.

She didn't express any worry that he might need more of his mother's attention than he was getting. I honestly think Tammy Faye didn't think she was worth much to anybody. It wasn't meanness that she didn't put him to bed every night, I think, but the feeling that she just didn't matter.

Some nights I put Jamie to bed, but some nights Vi Azvedo would do it.

Vi had had hard times in her life. She'd lost her first husband; and her young son, about twenty, had died suddenly—of a heart attack, or something like that.

She had remarried, a guy named Eddie who drove limousines for PTL. Eddie had had open-heart surgery, and he took life as it came. I thought of him as a good old boy.

Vi herself was not a dependently greedy person. I thought of her as a survivor. Wealth wasn't something she had to have.

A lot of people at PTL felt that Vi was responsible for putting the Bakkers' marriage back together after their separation, and for keeping it together. She was always with them, negotiating when they had a problem or a spat. She was the great mediator between Jim and Tammy.

The bottom floor of the Bakkers' house had a full kitchen that opened out onto the pool area. I often saw beer down there, but I never saw anybody drinking it. I don't know whose it was. Considering Jim's preaching against alcohol, it seemed odd to me that he allowed it in his house—before I saw him drinking vodka.

The pool was more or less kidney-shaped, with a footbridge going across its narrow waist.

The pool area was concrete and Astroturf. There were two gas grills, and some patio tables and chairs.

Down at the water's edge, there was a dock, with a walkway that connected to the boat house.

The dock was in a little cove of the lake, and Jim once told me to put up a line of floats and a No Trespassing sign across the mouth of the cove.

On weekends, the people from the area around the lake would get out in their boats, and after a few beers the guys would come into the cove. At the house we'd hear them call: "Bakker? Bakker!" A splash as a beer can hit the water. "Come on out here and walk on the water for us, Jimmy!"

This got on his nerves, and he wanted to keep them out of the cove.

I went over to Duke Power, but they said no way, it was a public lake.

After that, we'd just go out on the end of the dock and call softly, "Please, please. Mr. Bakker's taking a nap," sort of whispering loudly, and try to make them hush. Sometimes they would. Sometimes.

That was one of the very few ways the outside world brushed up against the house. It was insulated, you might say.

The house was staffed with round-the-clock guards, and two or three maids worked in the house each day. The guards were overseen by Don Hardister, and by me as the senior Security man around the property.

They were all on PTL payroll.

And they were in hot water with Tammy Faye all the time.

George was the guard on duty inside the house during the day, usually. Tammy Faye complained of him incessantly: he'd bought the wrong kind of groceries; he'd failed to clean the bird cages. George this, George that.

None of the family lifted a finger around that house. Yet Tammy Faye found it in herself to complain that the maids were folding her clothes wrong when they put them in her drawers.

Tammy Faye cooked twice that I remember. Once she made brownies. Once she made chocolate chip cookies. That was it.

She made huge amounts of each. I remember looking at the cookies, thinking there were enough for a
big first-grade class, if only we had the class, and the
milk to go with them. There were five pounds of
cookies there. And the brownies, too—she must have
made a hundred of them, far more than the household could possibly eat before they went bad.

Tammy Faye had always had a problem with rec-
ipe quantities for her family, because she'd learned
to cook from her mother, and her mother was cooking meals for a big household. She said in *I Gotta Be
Me* that when she and Jim were first married, "My
small meals would last Jim and me a whole week."

She still didn't have the hang of cooking in reason-
able quantities in 1984.

If the Bakkers didn't share much family life in the
evenings, they didn't do it in the mornings, either.

In the morning Jim would get all dressed and
ready to leave before he sat down to breakfast alone
in the breakfast nook, where George would have
set the table for him. It was very important that
George got it right; if Jim didn't find the table just
as he wanted it, it put him in a bad mood for the
day.

Jim liked food that he thought was good for him.
For breakfast he wanted to choose from a selection
of bran cereals, all set up in a specific order. A small
pitcher of milk, juice, and yogurt or fresh fruit completed his meal. Maybe he'd drink some water. Neither Jim nor Tammy Faye drank coffee.

Despite his wanting to eat a healthful diet, Jim had
a weakness for chocolate, and fudge, too. I took to
keeping chocolate-covered Granola bars in the car

for him. Jim worried a lot about keeping his slim figure, but he still ate the chocolate bars.

Sometimes at breakfast Jim would watch TV—he often caught a little of Jimmy Swaggart's morning program—and sometimes he wouldn't. He often seemed to be in deep thought. He'd make notes—never on a notepad, but on little pieces of scratch paper. He liked felt tip-pens, in unusual colors, and I began carrying one in the car in case he ever wanted one.

Tammy didn't eat breakfast with him. I think she usually got up later. I don't think she ate breakfast, usually. She probably started the day with a Tab. She was a Tab fanatic, always with one in her fist, wrapped in a tissue. If you saw a Tab on the counter and it had lots of lipstick on the top, you knew it was hers.

We had a crisis in 1984: the Coca-Cola company changed the formula on Tab, replacing the saccharin with Nutra Sweet. Tammy Faye told David to call the Coca-Cola company and tell them to make the old formula up in batches just for her! David didn't do it, and I don't blame him. Can't you hear what Coca-Cola would have said? "Listen, fella . . ."

We scurried around the area's stores, looking for the old-formula Tabs before they finished selling them. Finally we called the closest bottler and bought up his stock, too. We ended up squirreling away forty cases. They lasted until I was gone; heaven knows what she did the day *they* ran out!

The guards would get the kids up, give them breakfast, and take them to Heritage Academy, the Christian school at Heritage U.S.A.

Usually I waited outside for Jim, in the guardhouse, but I kept my eye peeled for that kitchen door. When Jim came out he expected me to be in the car, ready to roll. George helped; he'd let me know when Jim came in for breakfast.

Sometimes I'd kill some time playing with the family dogs.

In *I Gotta Be Me*, Tammy Faye wrote about the first dog her family ever had. He was "a tiny, black fuzzy puppy. Us kids about went crazy. We named him Smokey. . . . Smokey living with us gave me a love of animals.

"One hot day some kids came into our yard and a little boy knocked Smokey's water over. As a result Smokey bit the boy on the cheek. Mom . . . called my uncle who came and shot Smokey. When we got home, we found him in the garbage can. I thought I would die with grief. Part of my 'life' seemed to be in that garbage can.

"That night we had a funeral for Smokey. . . . We all cried and cried. . . . I still feel sad when I think of Smokey. . . ."

In 1984 the family owned three dogs. Two of them were Saint Bernards, big, heavily furred dogs that were miserable in the South Carolina summer.

While I was working for the Bakkers, Tammy went down to the York County Animal Shelter and brought home a third dog, a little white mutt. A Heinz 57, I called her.

Tammy named her Snuggles, and took her on the show one time. She would talk about Snuggles—"Ooh, Snuggles," she'd say, coming home at night.

Snuggles would come trotting up to the car, and Tammy would pat her.

Every now and then they'd take Snuggles in the house for a while, but not very often.

The guards looked after all the dogs. They fed them, and they did Snuggles's housebreaking at the guard shack.

The dogs were able to roam the neighborhood at will. They had a doghouse, but it wasn't fenced in.

The two Saint Bernards were good dogs, friendly and well-mannered, and Snuggles was a good dog, too. She looked funny, trotting along behind those two massive friends of hers.

As dogs will, they would leave the Bakker grounds, and we'd get irate calls from Tega Cay neighbors telling us to come get the dogs out of their gardens or they'd call the law on them.

Tega Cay had leash laws. I told Jim about them. He wanted to put a Cyclone fence around the property, but the city of Tega Cay would not allow it. He had trouble understanding that the city could tell him what to do. At the time I left, there was still no fence, although there is one now. The dogs were still running loose, and the guards were still getting calls.

Considering Tammy's feelings for Smokey, it seemed odd to me that neither she nor Jim spent any real time with the dogs.

But after all, I sometimes thought, Jim and Tammy didn't seem to have time for much of anything but spending money.

CHAPTER 11

Ask, and it shall be given unto you.
MATTHEW 7:7

The money Jim and Tammy spent was unbelievable unless you saw it.

In May 1984 they embarked on a spree of spending that began in New York City and ended in June in California.

We'd come from Minneapolis, where Jim had received an honorary doctorate from North Central Bible College, via Detroit, where we stayed in the Pontiac Sheraton, in the President's Suite on the top floor. It was a big suite, with three bedrooms as well as the master bedroom—plenty of room for Jim and Tammy, Jamie Charles and Tammy Sue, Vi Azvedo, David Taggart, and me. Vi roomed with Tammy Sue, Jamie Charles had a room and so did I and David. Tammy was very unhappy with the suite; it wasn't good enough.

I thought we were heading back to Charlotte, but all of a sudden plans were changed to include New York.

Luckily I'd packed enough clothes. You learned to do that with the Bakkers. If you were going on a two-day trip, the wise thing was to take enough clothes for ten, because you never knew when you'd really get home.

A limousine, which David Taggart had arranged, met us at La Guardia, and took us to the Waldorf Towers.

Our suite really impressed me. Once through the long hallway, you entered the sitting room, which had a baby grand, a fireplace, a large television, and lovely antique-looking furniture.

The dining room had a long, Queen Anne style table, big windows, and a very high ceiling. There was a complete kitchen. I slept in the "maid's room," which had its own bath.

On the other side of the suite there were three bedrooms. Jim and Tammy's was huge. Tammy Sue and Vi had the second bedroom, and David and Jamie shared the third.

It was evening when we arrived, and we ordered supper from downstairs. I said I'd like chicken salad. When the food came, somehow I found out that my chicken salad cost seventeen dollars! The crazy price made me so sick I could hardly eat.

The next day we went shopping.

At Saks, Jim bought a bunch of new suits, I think five, for about $900 apiece. Jim was hard to fit. He wore a 36-short coat, and that's so small it's hard to find.

David edited his clothes. As I've said, David had gorgeous clothes himself, and Jim trusted his taste, more, I sometimes thought, than Jim trusted his own.

David would pick out the suits he thought Jim should try on, and tell him whether they looked good.

David bought a pair of leather trousers for $400, and a pair of leather shorts for $200. And then he bought a pair of pajamas that astounded me.

They were linen, and they had short bottoms. They cost $700.

They looked to me like something you might buy in Belk's.

That purchase almost overshadowed for me the fact that Jim was spending $4000 on suits in one day—less than a week after buying all those clothes in Minneapolis.

Tammy Faye, Vi Azvedo, and Tammy Sue were shopping, too. Tammy was really into St. John's knits. She loved them—knit skirts and tops. They were, I think, $600 for an outfit. All three of the women bought a good many clothes.

We went to the Louis Vuitton store, where they bought a lot of stuff. I don't remember exactly what was in all those boxes I carried out, but Tammy bought a $200 key ring.

We went all over New York to find Jamie Charles a pair of leather pants, and he wanted a Michael Jackson coat and glove—remember Jackson's red coat and the glove on one hand? Nothing would do until Jamie had these. We finally found them, and bought them for about $200.

It was buy, buy, buy, all day long. My job was to carry things out to the limousine, and also to make sure they knew where to send things that were being delivered to the hotel.

In the late afternoon we went back to the suite,

and everybody started trying on and looking at what they had bought, and then we went out to eat at a little nearby restaurant.

After that, we went to see *A Chorus Line*. David had gotten the tickets from a scalper—they were over $100 a seat, or so he said.

It was quite an experience going to a Broadway show in a limousine.

When we pulled up in front, everybody looked at us getting out.

People recognized Jim, and other people recognized Tammy. I'd say it was about 50/50 which one they identified first. They seemed very friendly and pleased to see the Bakkers. New York received them very well all the time we were there. People would want to come up to talk to them, but of course I kept the people away, because that was how Jim and Tammy wanted it.

I liked *A Chorus Line*. A guy named Ben Harkey was in it at the time, and somehow David knew him. After the show Harkey and his wife came over to the suite and spent half the night, talking.

Harkey was a Christian, and he had a prayer group of actors. Later Jim had him come down to PTL and appear on the show.

I was miserable that night in the suite. The Harkeys' visit simply meant I couldn't go to bed yet—and I was exhausted.

We spent the rest of our week in New York shopping and shopping and shopping. One night we sandwiched in another show, *The Rink,* with Liza Minelli, also on high-priced tickets.

One day was different. David and Jim said that

they were going to a television station, and that they wouldn't need me.

I knew that a television station up there was owed a lot of money, and PTL was having some problems from them. I couldn't help thinking then that the money we were spending that week might have covered the overdue bill.

I think now they weren't going to a television station at all. Jim wouldn't have hesitated to take me on a trip to a station.

I think they went somewhere to see Jessica Hahn, or to some meeting about the Jessica Hahn incident, if I can call it that.

Aimee Cortese had met with Hahn earlier in the spring, or so the papers say in the summer of 1987.

And Aimee Cortese had left the suite with Jim and David. She had also visited the suite the night before. Tammy had groused about it. "Oh, why's *she* coming? I don't want to have her here." Tammy didn't dislike Aimee, she was just in a bad mood.

My mood was none too good, either. When I finally got off duty, usually after ten at night, I'd go into my little room and open the window, leaning on the windowsill to have a smoke. I'd look down at the streets far below, wishing I could be down there with the real people.

I've never felt lonelier in my life. The fantasy world of the Bakkers wasn't mine—but it was the world I was in.

It was an awful feeling.

We went back to Charlotte, but not for long. We stayed for no more than a couple of weeks—time for Jim to go on television begging for money for the

Heritage Grand, time to have the kitchen redecorated, and time to start people working on the new French doors and deck for their bedroom.

Then we left town again, this time for Palm Desert, California.

Jim had been in an awful mood since we got back from New York, and David was tough to be around then, too. David just wouldn't tell me where I was supposed to be when. It sometimes made things awkward for me.

I wasn't looking forward to the trip to Palm Desert, but I packed my things.

I was under the impression that we were going on a commercial airliner, but one day Taggart told me, "No. We'll be going on a private jet."

Johnnie the maid, Vi Azvedo, David Taggart, Jim and Tammy and the kids and I flew out in a Sabrejet with our own stewardess and pilot and copilot, with a nice meal on board.

In Palm Springs we were met by Vi's husband Eddie, who'd come out earlier to meet us. We'd rented a Lincoln Continental and a Cadillac. Eddie was in a Jeep Cherokee. Jim went over and got in the driver's seat of the Jeep.

He liked it, and said: "I have to get one of these." He bought one later.

We got everything loaded up and drove to Palm Desert.

The house was very nice, with a Spanish sort of look to it. When you walked through the front gate, you were in a little garden area, with a small pond. Beyond the large double doors was an immaculately furnished living room. It had been the model house for the development, and it was completely decorated and furnished. The living room had an off-white carpet, a white pit-type seating group, a large black table and chairs, a fireplace.

Jim and Tammy Faye's bedroom had sliding glass doors, through which you could see the bushes on the ledge that protected us from the house next door. The king-sized bed had a sand-colored bedspread, and the carpet and walls were light-colored, too. The room had a desk, a cabinet with a TV inside, and some artificial trees.

The house had a very nice kitchen, complete with china and glasses. Out in back was a pool and a large patio. There were three bedrooms altogether.

After we got the family moved in that evening, Vi gave Eddie a shopping list and money, about $350, and he and I went to the grocery store. We bought probably eight containers of Tropicana orange juice, about four gallons of milk, soft drinks, fruit, all kinds of sandwich meat, cereals, and cleansers and paper towels.

When we got back with the $300 worth of food, Tammy Faye had told Jim she wanted to go out that evening. We went to a place called Marie Callender's. Everybody went except Johnnie.

This was the night Tammy Faye described her diet plan: she and Jim ordered dessert first. She said that she tempted herself that way: she'd eat half, then keep it on the table to tempt herself with. How this was supposed to be a diet, I don't understand, but that's what she called it.

She and Jim generally tasted each other's food, and they'd pass it around to everybody.

The pies at Marie Callender's were really, really good. After dinner, Tammy decided she'd like to take some home. She stood by the big glass case, saying, one of those, two of those, two pumpkin, two coconut. Jim threw in an order for a pecan, and by the time we left we had ten or twelve pies.

Nobody ever ate them, just picked at them, and a few days later they were thrown out.

When we got back to the house Jim put on his blue bathing suit while David unpacked his clothes and set the shower up with his toiletries. Johnnie had already made the bed. Tammy put her bathing suit on, too. It was two-piece, aqua. That was the first time I saw her in a bathing suit.

She was gorgeous. Sexier than I had imagined. Her bare skin was smooth and tan, very well taken care of. Lust took me by surprise.

I was almost embarrassed by what I felt.

I think she knew what she did to me, because from then on she'd do things, consciously or unconsciously, that turned me on.

We never made love. I never even touched her, except to help her in or out of the car. But she put me through a lot of private hell out there in Palm Desert.

I'd watch Jim and Tammy disappear into their bedroom, and be jealous of him. I'd think, I see a woman he doesn't see.

That first night out there, when we finished moving the family in, David and Johnnie and Vi and Eddie and I went to the Rancho Las Palmas Motel for the night.

The next morning, about seven o'clock, we were

back at the house. Johnnie fixed fruit and cereal. Soon as Jim and Tammy had had breakfast, I expected they'd be busy; otherwise, why'd they make us come that early? But they sat around until nine o'clock. Then we began getting things the way they wanted them.

The house had gorgeous, very expensive plants, but they belonged to a florist, and the real estate man was insisting on getting them back. Jim and David wanted to keep them; they went to see about this the first morning. They lost—the plants had to go back.

The telephone wasn't hooked up yet. Vi Azvedo was supposed to have taken care of that sometime beforehand, or her husband Eddie, who'd come out ahead of us. Anyway, they hadn't done it. Jim didn't reproach her, but he just couldn't abide being without the phone.

I hated to see him get in a bad mood—it meant he'd be a terror the rest of the day. And then Tammy got mad about something in the kitchen, I forget what it was, but I could see it hurt Johnnie's feelings. I tried to comfort Johnnie, but I don't think it helped much.

Now the phone problem flowed downhill to me, and I was told the phone *had* to be hooked up that day. I went to the phone company and begged and pleaded, and we did get the hookup the same day. That made Jim happy. The first call he made was to Shirley Fulbright, to check on donations: "How many trays today, Shirley?"

Jim was uptight that day. I think he was bored. That day and the next, the show was one they'd made ahead. So he didn't have anything to concentrate on.

After their taped shows ran, during the rest of our stay the Bakkers usually spent mornings watching Reverend Dortch fill in as the host of the show. Jim and Tammy criticized details of his work as they watched, and Jim spent lots of time telling his secretary changes for the next day: more emphasis on selling Bibles, I remember, and more spots selling the Lifetime Partnerships. More selling, that's what he wanted. Jim made lots of these calls on the portable phone, while in the pool. He did a lot of work from the pool, now that I think of it.

Vi and Tammy Faye went shopping that first full day. I don't know what they bought; I wasn't there when they came back.

That evening the Bakkers said they were too tired to go out, so I went and got Kentucky Fried Chicken, four twenty-piece buckets, both the Crispy and the Original, and a lot of biscuits. We ate out near the pool.

They had some patio furniture out there, but Jim and Tammy Faye were very unhappy with it. It wasn't enough, and not the right kind.

By the time they let us go back to the motel, it was time to take a shower and go to bed.

Jamie Charles loved that pool, and spent all his time in it. Jim had a thing about the pool, that somebody had to be out there with Jamie—even though the pool wasn't deep enough to drown him, only about four feet. He could wade around in every part of it without ever getting over his head.

We kept that private plane and crew on standby for at least two days, in case they wanted to go somewhere else or they wanted to go back home. How much do you suppose that cost?

The next morning we heard that Tammy Faye had gotten scared the night before. She'd heard a noise, or something. She said that she'd thought I was staying there, and that she got up in the night and came looking for me to tell me about the noise, to get me to check it out, and had gotten real scared when she found out I wasn't there. She was pitching a fit. Jim was all bent out of shape, too.

That night I began staying at the house. Jamie Charles's room had a daybed, and that's where I stayed.

I really hated staying with them. They never gave me any free time. And this time, having to share a room with Jamie Charles . . . I liked him, but I was used to having my privacy, not rooming with a kid.

That day we went looking for all new dishes for the house, and also for glassware to fill a glass cabinet in the den. In the living room was a big black cabinet, black lacquer with glass doors, and we had to buy dishes to fill it.

As I've said before, the Bakkers had to have everything filled, and with something on it, and something around it, too.

The glassware was big black goblets, and the plates were white with black and gold trim. We must have spent four to five thousand dollars on those alone. We also bought a long runner for the hallway. I don't remember how much that was.

To tell you how much it was, it wouldn't all fit in the car. A truck had to follow us home from the store.

As soon as the stuff got home they began ripping

into the boxes, to see what all they'd bought. Like kids opening Christmas presents. That was their way.

They opened the boxes, but Johnnie and Vi and I washed all the plates and glasses. It was late in the afternoon by the time we had them clean and put in the cabinets.

That night—I think it was a Thursday—we ate at a place called Friday's. Tammy was wearing her white jumpsuit with white high heels. She looked breathtaking, despite her usual heavy makeup. Her skin had taken a golden color from the sun and she was letting her own hair show. Her zipper was pulled down to show lots of cleavage, and the jumpsuit had little ties at the ankles.

She got the first looks, and you could see people were making comments about her as they recognized her. She never seemed to mind people talking about her. Both she and Jim seemed very pleased that they were recognized.

Tammy ordered a salad, because of watching her weight; but by the size of that salad, no way she'd lose any.

Jim had been kicking around the idea that he wanted a Rolls-Royce. He and Tammy had had one before, in 1980; they had given it up because of the pressure of disapproval. But now Jim wanted another.

The next day we went out to the Rolls dealership in Palm Springs and looked at the cars, but he decided that he didn't want a new one. So David and I were told to find somebody in the area who dealt in old Rolls-Royces. We found a dealer in Santa Ana called Concannon's Horseless Carriages. Santa Ana is about a one-and-a-half-hour drive across some mountains from Palm Desert.

We made plans to go over there the next day. I thought we were going to use the Cadillac we had rented, but we would not be driving: Taggart said the three-hour drive would take too much of Jim's time. We were going to fly.

The next morning David rented a plane. The only one he could find was a Learjet. Tammy Faye had been thinking about going with us, but when she found out it was a Learjet, she wouldn't go. A Learjet fuselage is quite tight, and Tammy Faye said she was liable to claustrophobia.

But I think Tammy didn't really mind not going along. She wanted to go shopping for clothes. She was putting a California wardrobe together, one she could leave at the Palm Desert house. So David and Jim and I went to Santa Ana.

It must have struck Jim as an irony that he was going to Santa Ana to buy a Rolls.

It was in Santa Ana that Jim and Paul Crouch had started up Channel 46, from applying for the license on up, after Jim had left Pat Robertson.

There had been no money to spare in those days. Jim was fond of telling the story of the onetime computer building that they were going to renovate as a television studio. Here's how he told it in *Move that Mountain*:

" 'There is one problem,' Tammy was eyeing the floors.

" 'Yep, I can see that tile will have to come up,' I said. 'Television cameras need a flat, hard surface. We could never get them across this.'

"Tammy and Paul's wife, Jan, charged into the job of removing the tile. Dressed in a Mickey Mouse T-shirt, Tammy made an interesting sight. The tile popped off easily enough, but underneath was a thick layer of tar. Puzzled at how to finish the job, the girls' work came to a stop. Minutes later, Duane Riddle, a local Assembly of God associate pastor, walked in with his wife.

" 'I've got just the chemical you need to dissolve that stuff,' he said. 'I'll be right back with it.'

"After one application, the hardened tar became a sea of black mud as the chemical began loosening it. Ultimately, Tammy began wading out into the 'sea' and scooping the black mess into big garbage cans lined with plastic bags. When the job was finished, everybody involved with the project looked like the 'tar baby' from the Uncle Remus stories."

And now Jim was flying back to Santa Ana in a Learjet!

It was about a seven-minute flight.

In Santa Ana we were met by a limousine from Concannon's. The company had about forty or fifty cars at the time, so we just started looking. Finally Jim picked out two that he wanted to ride in. One was blue, some kind of Shadow, I think. It had belonged to Walt Disney. Jim modeled a lot of the stuff he did at PTL on Walt Disney. Disney was kind of a hero to Jim, and Jim both admired him and was determined to outdo him. He came pretty close. In 1987, Heritage U.S.A. was right behind Disney World and Disneyland in popularity.

Unfortunately, Concannon's had a prior commitment on the Disney car; we couldn't buy it. So we moved back to a 1953 Rolls, I think it was. It was burgundy and had a brown leather interior. It was beautiful. Jim rode in it and liked it, so they bought it.

They gave about $57,000 for it.

We arranged to have it delivered to Palm Desert, and flew back across the mountains to Palm Desert.

The next day, Jim and all of us went to look for a Mercedes, and they bought Tammy Faye a 450SL. They gave right at $50,000 for it. In two days: over $100,000 spent on cars.

But they weren't through buying on this trip. That night we went to an auction in Palm Desert and spent over $6,000 on bronzes by the Western artist Frederick Remington. They bought four or five, all the Remingtons on sale that night, almost like buying postcards or something. They wanted them for the new house. And Tammy Faye bought some jewelry and stuff.

Let me go back to Concannon's for a moment. While we were there, they also bought a black Rolls-Royce that Jim wanted to put on display at the hotel. This is the car that couldn't be located in the spring of 1987; I read in the newspapers that it had finally been found, still at Concannon's, undergoing restorations.

Jim and David were doing a lot of talking about the buying of this second Rolls, and I got the impression that they were planning the purchase of the second car to justify buying the first car in some way—but it was a confusing conversation, and I may have misunderstood.

Not long after this, *The Charlotte Observer* found

out that they had bought the one (burgundy) Rolls-Royce in California.

In private, Jim was beginning to hate the paper. He told me that Knight-Ridder, the chain that owned it, was run by atheists and wanted to attack Christ through him. He said the paper had told him that they'd sworn to get him, and they had the money to put a reporter on him full-time until they'd destroyed him. He was really angry at the paper, and the media in general.

Jim even preached against the press. In a 1985 sermon, he said: "Where there is no talebearer there is no strife. . . . It is the talebearer that goes to the newspaper. Many times it is the newspaper reporter that's a talebearer. That's what reporting is, it's talebearing. Whenever a minister falls into sin . . . it is . . . the talebearing that tears their lives apart, and many times they can never go back into the pulpit. Not because of the sin as much as because of the talebearer. You don't like that because you got to take it upon yourself. . . . For love hardly notices when others do it wrong, and love covers a multitude of S-I-N, sin, sin, sin. . . . So where there is no talebearer, the strife ceases. That's where the strife is, folks. It's in the gossip, it's in the talking about it. Just remember the Italian saying, 'Shutta your mouth!' If you don't remember anything else from this sermon, just remember 'Shutta your mouth!' "

It's an odd way of looking at which matters more: the sin, or the uncovering of the sin. But it was Jim's.

I remember Jim talking to me one time in front of the Heritage Grand Hotel. He asked me what I thought of the way *The Charlotte Observer* treated him.

I said, "Jim, leave the newspaper alone. If what you are doing is right, you have nothing to worry about."

He didn't say anything.

Jim handled the *Observer's* finding out about the car in his usual way: he used the show to tell the Partners about it—his way.

On television Jim said that he felt like he deserved the personal Rolls, that he had worked so hard and that he and Tammy Faye had bought it with their own money.

Not more than three months earlier, I heard him tell a staff meeting that the ministry was in such bad financial shape that he and Tammy had put all their savings back into it. Yet they had the money to go out and spend $100,000 on cars!

By the middle of my stay in Palm Desert, I was starting to see more and more clearly what they were doing. They were just relentlessly spending money. They bought three TVs for the house. Tammy and Vi came in almost every day with armfuls of new clothes, new pocketbooks (Tammy's favorites were Louis Vuitton and Gucci), shoes, gold chains, fake diamond rings, other jewelry. They were buying a California wardrobe for Tammy Sue, too. It was no matter to them that the ministry was again getting in bad financial shape, spending more money each month than it was taking in, millions more.

This Palm Desert car buying, coming on top of the New York spending frenzy and the Minneapolis spree, just really made it hard for me to see how they could justify their life-style to their Partners or to the

American people. But then, Jim often often said he didn't care what the public thought of him, as long as his Partners backed him.

In all that time, I did hear Jim say sometimes, "We need to cut back on manpower"—but I never once heard him say, "We need to cut back on the expenses of the president's office," or refer to trimming their personal indulgences. Not once.

I don't know how they could justify their life-style to themselves, come to that, although perhaps David Taggart and Vi Azvedo helped them. David and Vi would tell them that they had done so much good for people, and had built so much, that nothing was too good for them. I think Jim and Tammy had been told this enough that they had started to believe it.

I was starting to question myself, and I was beginning not to feel good about the answers. I was seeing too much, and I was living too much, of the good life. I was starting to question myself hard for even being there, but I still thought that maybe I was just tired—and I was very tired—and was just wrong about what I was seeing. Jim did so many good things . . . people loved him so. . . .

In July, when PTL was thinking about buying its own jet, David Taggart said to me one day, "Do you know how much we paid for that plane trip to California and back? $120,000."

I almost dropped my teeth. We could all have flown out there and back for under $5000.

He went on, "That's not all. Do you know how much it cost us to fly from Palm Desert to Santa Ana and back? $3,000."

I shook my head. My stomach was turning over. I

felt guilty to be associated with this, even though I had no responsibility in the matter. I was just there for the ride, you might say. But by July it was getting harder and harder for me to weigh the good against the bad and have the good win out.

In Palm Desert, I'd just been tormented by Tammy Faye's sexiness. She could always find a sexy meaning in remarks where none was intended, but out there I was more conscious of that than usual.

Back at PTL, I had been seeing a lovely lady. I made sure the Bakkers didn't know about her, because I wanted my privacy.

Out in Palm Desert I was very lonely.

I'm sure that's one reason why I went through so much torment over Tammy Faye.

But she helped.

She'd come out to that pool area in one or another bathing suit, looking terrific, and then she'd lie down on a chair. I remember this happening once when I was alone out there. I got up to go inside as fast as I could, but she wouldn't let me go.

"No, stay, Mike. You don't have anything you have to do right now, do you?"

She pulled out that suntan oil and began stroking it onto her arms.

I had no choice. I had to stay.

I couldn't keep my eyes off her.

I couldn't look at her.

I have no idea what we talked about. The weather, maybe? Something like that.

It felt like years before I was able to get away. Or

maybe I should say, it felt like years before I could make myself get away.

Every minute of that stay in Palm Desert I was conscious of her as a very desirable woman.

How much of that was her doing, I have no idea.

I just know how I felt.

It was miserable.

In the summer PTL bought itself two toys.

One was its own jet. Richard Dortch found the plane and engaged the crew. PTL hired two pilots full-time. I guess it gave PTL some kind of big status to have the plane. It was hangared out at the Charlotte airport.

I guess maybe it put a stop to things like the $120,000 expense we'd run up on our spring trip to Palm Desert. There was that much to say for it, anyway.

The other toy was a miniature train. It was a copy of an 1864 train, only smaller, of course. Jim talked about the train at the St. Louis zoo; he was determined that his train would be better. Whatever he had, it had to be the *best*.

It would run on a track in front of the Partner Center, which was still unfinished, out to the Water Park, which they were then planning to build.

Special workers came in to get special cross ties made, and the track laid, but the work wasn't going as fast as Jim wanted.

When about thirty feet of track was laid, Jim had to have the engine brought out and put on the track.

He'd go out there every day and play on it. Back it up twenty feet, and bring it forward.

Of course Partners and other people visiting PTL would come down there and watch him. It embarrassed me, it was so undignified, but that didn't trouble Jim. He took to wearing an engineer cap and his blue jeans, and he'd have pictures taken.

Every day they'd lay a little more track, and every day he'd go out and play on the train.

At last the track was finished, but Jim didn't stop playing with the train. He'd ride it all around the track, and give free rides.

The train is still there, and I think people like it a lot.

Once Jim calmed down about the train, he wanted a trail bike.

Jim, by the way, was a lousy athlete, other than being a good roller skater. I played tennis with him once, but he gave up and we left.

Anyway, he wanted a trail bike. The next thing you know, we were down at the Honda place buying one.

Jim said they were going to start building a trail bike course down on the property. There certainly wasn't one at the time.

Jim took to riding the bike every day out through the woods. I didn't have a bike, but I borrowed Don Hardister's so that I could go with Jim, and sometimes Don came with us too, in which case I'd borrow another one.

Jim would ride out there for hours at a time. He was not too good at first, not too coordinated, but he kept getting a little bit better.

Jim's interest in the bike lasted a couple of months. But Don Hardister wrecked his bike one afternoon and had to be taken to the hospital, and that evidently scared Jim. He didn't get back on his bike much after that.

That was a relief to David Taggart, who had been ticked off about the bike—he'd lose his temper trying to find Jim for scheduled meetings and other work, only to discover he was out on the bike.

It was in the summer that David said one day, "Hey, I've got something to tell you."

"What?"

"Tammy Faye thinks that you're on drugs."

"*What?!* She thinks that *I'm* on drugs?!" I mean, me knowing that she is taking Valium like it is going out of style, and here she is accusing me!

When I was alone with Jim, I brought it up: "Let's clarify something right now. This kid here does not take drugs. Never has and never will. I don't take any kind of drugs. I just want to clarify that."

He seemed shocked that I was even bringing it up.

I have only one explanation for why Tammy might have gotten that idea into her head.

Since my return from Palm Desert in June, I'd managed to get my attraction to Tammy Faye under control. I didn't react to her that powerfully any more. Perhaps she missed it.

The Bakkers never knew that I was seeing a lady, and both Jim and Tammy would make a to-do about getting me into a serious dating relationship.

Tammy was after me very frequently about not having a girl, and kept suggesting this or that PTL woman as suitable: "So-and-so's pretty, Mike. You ought to go after her." And she'd touch me on the arm.

Jim was always bemoaning my apparent unattached state: "I'll get you fixed up; I'll look after you."

And I'd say, "Well, Jim, let me ask you: When do you give me time to womanize? By the time you let me off work, I'm too tired to be any good to a woman. I've got to go home and go to sleep."

"You have to make time for things like that," he'd answer blithely.

One night when Jim addressed an all-woman singles seminar, he really got my goat.

As he was finishing, he said to them, "And by the way, this is my bodyguard, Mike Richardson. He's single and available."

I nearly dropped my teeth. I didn't know where to look. I wanted out of there, in the fastest way.

As we headed out, Jim was looking smug and unconcerned.

I was trotting along, for once almost as fast as he was. I yelped, "What are you *doing* to me, Jim?! There's two hundred women out there!"

Jim was grinning. "Aren't you available, Mike?"

I spread my hands, outdone with him. The lady I was seeing was there, listening, although of course he didn't know that. I was surrounded by trouble. She told me later it was a good thing I didn't nod my head.

He grinned more widely. "Do you want me to be your bodyguard, Mike?"

I was dying. "No, we'll just sneak out of here. Now. Fast."

He told Tammy about it later, and she cracked up, laughing at me. "You ought to have been able to take your pick, Mike!"

I laugh, now, thinking about it. Jim got me good that night, I guess.

PTL people tended to date within PTL—it was hard for an outsider to understand what PTL people talked about, their world was so different. People watched one another like hawks. There seemed to me to be more interest in others' sexual lives than you'd find in the average small community of 3,000.

I knew who the wife-swappers had been, as I told you, and three of the four people had been PTL employees. Two of them still were.

Although Jim had put a stop to the practice, he had not fired any of them. One couple was still together in 1984, although they have now divorced, and the man, at least, has remarried. The other couple had split up, and the man had left PTL, but the wife was still there. She was dating, of course. She was very attractive, with a gorgeous, lush figure, but I never asked her out.

I wasn't interested in starting any more friendships at PTL. By the summer, I was interested in getting out.

CHAPTER 12

Write the things which thou hast seen
REVELATIONS 1:19

In Palm Desert, I was starting to question myself, and I was beginning not to feel good about myself. I was seeing too much.

I was seeing the way Jim and Tammy were spending money, and the way they used the people they should have valued.

They lived a two-part life. They said they cared. They said they loved God and people, and wanted to make sure things were done right for the people of God—and then they were turning right around and absolutely throwing away money on things that they did not even need.

I was very tired by then. And I was still caught up in looking at the good things Jim and Tammy did, still trying to say they outweighed the bad.

It was getting harder all the time.

Then there would be a kindness, and I'd hesitate again.

It was very kind of PTL to give me that $1000 bonus, for instance, and kind of David Taggart, too.

And daily there were people on the PTL staff who did good things for people, people who truly respected the Partners, who loved the good ministry that was taking place there. More and more through the summer I found myself watching those good people, leaning on their example, drawing strength from them to keep going.

But Jim and Tammy were living the television screen one way and their private lives another. I couldn't handle it.

I just couldn't handle it.

I'd think about Jim and Tammy: what would make them happy, peaceful people? I didn't reach any happy conclusions.

Tammy Faye was happiest, when I knew her, when she was performing—either at the mike or behind the puppet curtain—but she wasn't fully easy even then. The ministry had, I think, gotten too big for her. But that year there was another barrier between her and happiness: her feelings were a roller coaster. She couldn't keep control of herself, much less anything around her. She'd come from such humble beginnings to so much money and fame— but now she seemed very dependent on the money and fame. I don't think she could have been happy in a humble ministry, either. Not anymore.

And Jim? Jim, it struck me, would never be able to say, "I've done what I set out to do." There would always be one more building to build, one more ministry to start, one more dollar to bring in.

Reaching these conclusions didn't make me happy.

And Jim kept bringing in the money; not just one more dollar, either. By August Jim had now gone up to asking for $2500 and $5000 donations.

During the summer I had become friends with a man who worked for Bell South Advertising and Publishing Corporation (BAPCO). He offered me a job selling Yellow Pages in North Carolina. I went down and passed the test required. My friend said it would be a couple of weeks before I heard exactly when the company would want me to start work.

In the last week of September Jim had given me a couple of days off, and I went down to Savannah, Georgia, to see my mother. My nerves were about shot. I hadn't had any rest for almost a year.

Then I received a call from David Taggart: Jim was going back to California, and I had to meet them in Atlanta no later than 1:57 that afternoon, when their plane was landing.

I had the job at Bell South, but I had no way of knowing how long it would be before I could start over there.

I was torn between going to California and resigning right then—but it seemed to me I'd better go.

There was a flight leaving Savannah at 12:00 noon, arriving in Atlanta at 1:00 or 1:15.

I threw everything in a bag and ran.

In Atlanta I had about thirty minutes total to find Jim's gate. I didn't know why they were flying commercial, since the jet was so new, but I found out later: a TV crew had been flown out ahead of time to Palm Desert on the PTL jet, and Jim didn't want to ride with them.

Well, in Atlanta, I stopped to call a girl I had been

201

seeing in Charlotte, to see how she was, and to see whether BAPCO had called—I'd given them her number to call while I was in Savannah.

"Mike," she said, "you got a call from Bell South this morning and they need to know by three o'clock whether you are going to take the job.

Three o'clock! I'd be in the plane to California a lot longer than that.

I'd have to call right now, or let the job go.

I called Bell South.

Busy signal.

Again I called.

Busy.

Again.

Busy.

I had fifteen minutes left to locate Jim's gate and get myself over there.

Busy.

And then I got through.

The personnel lady answered, and I told her I was taking the job.

"Well," she said, "can you come by tomorrow and do some things?"

"No, ma'am, I am on my way to California. I'm in the Atlanta airport right now."

She asked me to come in one day in the next week.

I tried to explain to her that I didn't know how long I'd have to be out in California. As I've said before, you never knew how long the Bakkers would keep you out on the road—and how could I promise her a day next week? All I could think about was the clock.

It was ticking on to 1:45.

"Well, when can you start?"

"When am I supposed to start?"

She said, "October fifteenth."

I said, "I'll take the job. I've got to go now."

I hung up and ran to the nearest monitor.

The Bakkers' gate was twenty-five gates away.

I hustled up and reached the gate just about the time the plane was landing.

I was glad to see Jim and Tammy, in a way. They had never wronged me personally, never done anything to hurt me. I felt more sorry for them than anything else. I just couldn't live with the things they lived with, the things they did.

We caught the plane west, and arrived in Palm Desert.

I thought back on the private torment I'd felt on our last visit; I was over that, now.

The next day or two we did some filming, a lot of commercials and spots to be used back on the show in Fort Mill, and then the TV crew was ready to go.

I found out at five in the afternoon that they were going to leave on the private jet at about eight o'clock that night.

For the next few hours I was in such a stew. Could I go to Jim and tell him I was quitting? He might be nice, and let me fly back. But he was just as likely, I knew now, to tell me I could walk home—and it was three thousand miles. In any case, he would want to hear all about why I was quitting, and I was in no shape to tell him.

Around seven o'clock I caught Jim and said that I needed to go back home. My stepfather was sick, and was scheduled for a small operation. This was indeed true. I added what wasn't true: "I feel like I need to be there."

Jim said, "Fine."

The crew was loading their stuff in the van for the airport. I ran and grabbed my things, said my good-byes, jumped in the van, and caught the plane back to Charlotte.

I went straight to PTL where I sat down and wrote up a resignation.

In it I told Jim and Tammy that I cared a lot about both of them and the kids and had grown real close to them. And I had. I really had—there was no doubt of that. But, I went on, I felt that I had to pursue other interests of mine, and I hoped that they would forgive me for leaving. I added that I wished them the best of luck.

I left my resignation on Don Hardister's desk and left.

The next day I talked to Don.

I was due enough vacation time to cover the days until I would start at Bell South, so I didn't actually work for PTL any more. I almost wrote, "so I was through with PTL." But that wouldn't be true.

I will never be "through" with PTL. It had a tre-mendous effect on my life.

Before, I'd see a drunk lying in the gutter and have nothing but contempt for him.

Now I wonder what happened to that guy to put him there.

Now I thank God that I am as fortunate as I have been. I guess, on his good days, Jim taught me some-thing.

But then there were the things that I saw at PTL,

and the suffering that I saw. The people who would give their last dimes to try to make that organization go—they believed in it. It was their dream.

The dream that Jim Bakker sold them. . . .

I will never get over my year at PTL as long as I live.

EPILOGUE

A time to get, and a time to lose; a time to keep, and a time to cast away

ECCLESIASTES 2:6

On June 29, 1987, I returned to Heritage U.S.A. It was my first visit since leaving the Charlotte area in late 1984.

I didn't make my visit alone, although there was no one in the car with me. I rode with Jim, with memories and voices flooding my heart.

I passed the Billy Graham Home, and I could hear Jim's voice, delivering that comforting eulogy for Brad Lacey.

And sure enough, just as Jim had said, Brad was with me now.

To the right, near the gate, was where Jim had wanted to build an emergency medical facility. "It isn't just for PTL, Mike. This area really needs an emergency clinic." He was right. He'd add: "I want it open twenty-four hours. How many lives we could save! If we'd had it now, maybe we could have saved Brad."

I passed the PTL Home, and I was back there in that fool Victory March, capering along behind Jim, feeling like an idiot, unable to keep from grinning.

The Welcome Center—he'd loved building that place: "This is where they're going to get the full meaning of PTL. I've got to have staff here that are good with people. This place will always be clean and neat and orderly. The lobby of PTL."

Once it opened, he'd visit it at least once a week, and he always checked both restrooms himself. They had to be *spotless.* At the ladies' room door he'd call, "Anybody in there?" and look back at me with an embarrassed grin—but his embarrassment didn't stop him. In he'd go.

Once there was mud on the carpet and he went berserk: "Why hasn't this been cleaned? I've told you and told you this is the image center for Heritage U.S.A.—why is this dirty?"

A worker gave him the one answer that always satisfied him: "Mr. Bakker, we'll clean it immediately." He didn't want reasons or excuses, he just wanted it done, his way, right now.

I passed the real estate office, and once again Jim and I were going in to V. J. Sherk's office.

Jim: "V. J., sold anything today?"

"Yeah, Mr. Bakker. We're *always* selling stuff."

"We need to sell, sell, sell."

And I remembered Jim saying once outside V. J.'s office: "Maybe I should move Security down here. Then I could keep an eye on all you guys."

I drove past Lake Park Place, and heard Jim saying again: "I'm going to build me a house on the lake, build it into the far side of that bank under the trees."

I drove on past Lake Park Place, where no buildings stand.

At Mulberry Village I went back to when we were building the first model. Jim was fussing again about the landscaping and the interior decoration.

Christmas City wasn't up now, in June, but I saw it anyway, and Jim, so excited: "If only I could have seen stuff like this when I was a kid!" He was twisting around in his seat, looking, each time like the very first time: "Stop. I want to look at that." And we'd stop so he could look at one of those big gingerbread men—"It almost makes you feel like a little kid again, doesn't it, Mike?"

It did, I remembered that hot June day. It did make me feel like a kid again. It was wonderful. I loved him for making Christmas City. It was like a sweet dream come true.

And I remembered how the staff would complain at all the extra work of getting the City ready. And how I'd say, angrily, "He's the reason you're here, he's the reason you have a job, if you don't like what's demanded right now, then quit!" These words sure turned themselves on me. They had hurt a lot when I was trying to make myself leave. And in June they still hurt.

The Meadows Apartments, and Jim was back in the passenger seat, showing me where they were going to go, telling me exactly what they'd look like: and there they are.

Off Angel Boulevard, only a few people were working on the still unfinished Towers. If he were here, I thought, there'd be fifty times that many workers. . . .

I parked and went into Main Street, Jim's street of shops under a sky-blue roof, a sky with little electric stars in it. A couple in their twenties caught my eye, and I wondered if they could have any idea of the grief Jim went through to get the street just right. He must have ripped it up two or three times. . . .

I passed the Tammy Faye cosmetic shop, and I could grin again: I hope nobody'll ever model her makeup after Tammy Faye's. . . .

And the fudge shop. Jim loved chocolate. "People will like it," he said.

I went out and looked over at the Water Park. A couple of thousand people were there. It looked just like his little model. It was just like he had said it would be—a place people would love.

Except the wave pool wasn't working. He'd made such a to-do about that, in the planning.

And the train station. Him and his train! And it had to be coming down the track, full of happy people, and happy people were lined up to get on, every age from two to eighty. It was just as he'd said it would be.

I went over the bridge to the rotunda, where I did the chin-ups and Jim just shook his head. The rotunda stood half-built for so long; it's complete now.

In the gift shop, I asked where the Water Park offices were; I was meeting a friend there. The polite, kindly young woman told me, offered to phone ahead, and said: "You just tell the lady at the gate I said to let you in!"

I knew the motherly, older lady at the gate. Her name was Pauline; I didn't remember the rest of it.

She broke into a big smile at the sight of me. "Brother Richardson! You're back!"

"You remember me, Pauline?"

"Of course I do. It's so good to have you back!"

I went on through the gate, feeling awful. I wasn't back, not the way she thought; I didn't want to tell her that. I felt very lonely.

I met my friend, and the first words out of my mouth were: "Why isn't the wave pool working?" I heard what I'd said and couldn't believe it. I'd sounded just like Jim.

"You noticed that, did you? The hydraulics are broken, and we don't have the money to fix them, so we're pretending there's nothing wrong."

Later, alone again, I went to the studio, and parked where we used to, trying to pull myself together.

The memories of good things were just killing me, even with all I knew, and have told you, about the bad things.

The Upper Room looked just the same. Suddenly Vi was with me again, asking me to volunteer on the prayer phones.

The amphitheater, and I was back at the first performance of the Passion Play. That night the amphitheater was full of people, lights, music; full of life.

Today the amphitheater was empty.

But I was full of emotion.

Jim had done so much that was good. I'd seen him make good dreams become realities.

In the beginning I'd admired him. I'd admired his ministry.

Now, in 1987, with the results of his 1984 actions becoming clearer and clearer every day, I began to understand my year with Jim and Tammy in a different way.

I realized for the first time that I had not been wrong to believe in Jim Bakker. I had not failed.

Bakker had failed me.

Bakker had failed all of us.

We who believed did not have anything to be ashamed of.

PTL was not Jim and Tammy Bakker. PTL was everyone else. PTL was built by the blood, sweat, and tears of thousands, no, millions of good, honest, humble people who let Jim and Tammy Bakker be a part of their ministry.

It was not the other way around, as Bakker had wanted us to believe.

Bakker had tried to make people feel that they were not as good as he was, that we were low in the eyes of God and he was God's chosen one.

But we were better than he was: our commitment to PTL had been honest.

At last I went to the Outreach Center, and parked by the rear doors as I had so often. The first thing I'd do was get the door key in my hand, and then I'd trot to the doors, trying to beat him there.

He was a fast mover, one of the fastest I ever saw. And he hated to be stopped once he was in motion.

He's stopped now, I thought. I wanted to ask him why it had to happen this way.

What a lot of waste.

MIKE RICHARDSON (b. 1952) grew up in Conway and Charleston, S.C. After graduating from high school, he served in the Marine Corps for two years. He is a graduate of the University of South Carolina and the University of Louisville/Southern Police Institute.

After leaving PTL he worked with Bell South Advertising and Publishing Corporation for two years. He is now employed by a soft drink company in Charleston, S.C.